////// NASCAR®

HOT PURSUIT

Wendy Etherington

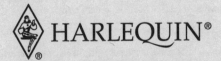

HARLEQUIN®

TORONTO • NEW YORK • LONDON
AMSTERDAM • PARIS • SYDNEY • HAMBURG
STOCKHOLM • ATHENS • TOKYO • MILAN • MADRID
PRAGUE • WARSAW • BUDAPEST • AUCKLAND

ISBN-13: 978-0-373-21795-3
ISBN-10:   0-373-21795-1

HOT PURSUIT

Copyright © 2008 by Harlequin Books S.A.

Wendy Etherington is acknowledged as the author of this work.

NASCAR® and the NASCAR Library Collection are registered trademarks of the National Association for Stock Car Auto Racing, Inc.

www.eHarlequin.com

Printed in U.S.A.

//////NASCAR

SECRETS and LEGENDS

HOT PURSUIT
by Wendy Etherington

From the opening green flag at Daytona to the final checkered flag at Homestead, the competition will be fierce for the NASCAR Sprint Cup Series championship.

The **Grosso** family practically has engine oil in their veins. For them racing represents not just a way of life but a tradition that goes back to NASCAR's inception. Like all families, they also have a few skeletons to hide. What happens when someone peeks inside the closet becomes a matter that threatens to destroy them.

The **Murphys** have been supporting drivers in the pits for generations, despite a vendetta with the Grossos that's almost as old as NASCAR itself! But the Murphys have their own secrets... and a few indiscretions that could cost them everything.

The **Branches** are newcomers, and some would say upstarts. But as this affluent Texas family is further enmeshed in the world of NASCAR, they become just as embroiled in the intrigues on and off the track.

The **Motor Media Group** are the PR people responsible for the positive public perception of NASCAR's stars. They are the glue that repairs the damage. And more than anything, they feel the brunt of the backlash....

These NASCAR families have secrets to hide, and reputations to protect. This season will test them all.

Dear Reader,

Okay, I'll admit it—I'm obsessed with NASCAR racing.

While friends and family talk about RBIs, linebackers and serving aces, I listen politely, usually having little idea what they're talking about. But you mention tires, engines, speed and checkered flags, and I'm riveted.

And since racing is naturally dramatic, emotional and filled with competition and conflict, it lends itself easily to storytelling. I hope you enjoy your peek into some of the people behind the scenes in my book, as well as the rest of the stories in Harlequin's officially licensed NASCAR romance series.

I'd love to hear from you (though I'm unavailable most Sunday afternoons). You can contact me through my Web site, www.wendyetherington.com, or through regular mail at P.O. Box 3016, Irmo, SC 29063.

Let's go racing!

Wendy Etherington

WENDY ETHERINGTON

was born and raised in the deep South—and she has the fried chicken recipes and NASCAR ticket stubs to prove it. Though a voracious reader since childhood, she spent much of her professional life in business and computer pursuits. Finally giving in to those creative impulses, she began writing, and in 1999 she sold her first book.

She has been a finalist for many awards—including the Booksellers' Best Award and several *Romantic Times BOOKreviews* awards. In 2006 she was honored by Georgia Romance Writers as the winner of the Maggie Award.

She writes full-time (when she's not watching racing) from her home in South Carolina, where she lives with her husband and two daughters.

To race fans past and present

REARVIEW MIRROR:

Ever since Hilton Branch skipped town with his bank's money, his sons—NASCAR drivers Bart and Will Branch—have been badgered by reporters more interested in Hilton's disappearance than the twins' qualifying efforts. Well, rumor has it that bounty hunters are on Hilton's trail and getting closer by the minute to locating him.

CHAPTER ONE

KYLIE PALMER strode briskly into her house, dropping her briefcase in the hall as she moved toward the bottom of the stairs. "Hey, champ!" she yelled. "Mom's home."

Her ten-year-old son, Ryan, darted out of his room with one sock on and one dangling from his hand. "Mom!" He ran down the stairs. "You're home early."

Kylie got a quick hug before he rounded the corner into the kitchen, probably in search of a snack. The boy was a bottomless pit these days.

"Ten minutes before we gotta go to soccer practice," he said.

Knowing she had to trade changing out of her pantsuit and heels for a ten-minute conversation with her never-slow-down son, she followed him and sat at the kitchen table. "Then I made it just in time."

In the process of smearing peanut butter on a piece of bread, Ryan turned. "You're taking me?"

"Unless your personal chauffeur is planning to show up and drive."

He frowned. "Are you talking about Honey, or are you just being funny?"

"I was going for funny."

"Yeah?" He turned back to his sandwich. "I think you missed the green flag on that one."

Kylie smiled. He was always better at humor than her. Like his father had been.

When she'd lost her policeman husband four years ago, the humor and understanding in Ryan's bright blue eyes had kept her going. The knowledge that she had to keep going forward for him had forced her to make her body move daily, trying to be both parents instead of half of a loving, unbeatable team.

As her mother was also a widow—and pretty bossy—Kylie had been informed rather quickly that she *couldn't* raise her son alone, so Kylie and Ryan had left the only home he'd ever known in the suburbs of Charlotte and had moved into her mother's grand lake house in Mooresville, North Carolina. The amazing view of Lake Norman notwithstanding, no mortgage payments and her mother's crazy optimism were blessings among her grief that she never took for granted.

"Where's Honey?" she asked Ryan.

"In the media room. I taught her how to play the racing game, and now she thinks she's gonna win the NASCAR Sprint Cup." He rolled his eyes with the put-upon, but somehow sweet, affection a boy his age had for "old people."

Not that her mother—who refused to be called "Grandma" and settled on the more hip "Honey" just after Ryan was born—would ever consider herself old. She looked great, felt great and moved with more ease than most twenty-year-olds.

Kylie wished she had her energy. She knew she accomplished things every day, but she often felt that each step became more and more difficult. She lacked motivation unless the task involved her son, and even then there were days that his boundless energy simply exhausted her. She'd recovered from the depression she'd sunk into after Matt's death, but now she was stuck in the middle. Not sad. Not happy.

It was almost worse.

"I'm ready for Daytona!" her mother, Madeline "Honey" Richardson, announced as she waltzed into the room.

So maybe Ryan's humor hadn't just come courtesy of his father's genes.

"Whafjush plaureh did youfisl carud in?" Ryan asked around a mouthful of peanut butter sandwich.

"Chew first, then talk," Kylie suggested, heading to the fridge to get the milk jug. She poured him a glass, and after he'd swallowed both, he tried again.

"What place did you come in?" he asked Honey.

Honey planted her hands on her trim hips. "First. What else?"

Ryan's eyes widened. "No way! I set the level to expert."

"Well, I did so—" She broke off, narrowing her eyes. "What do you mean you set the level to expert? I thought you said you were going to make it easy for my first time out?"

Obviously caught, Ryan's face reddened. "I did—

at first. But then you… Well, you…um, seemed to get the hang of it, so I made it harder, you know, to see how you'd hold up."

Honey shook back her trademark cap of honey-blond curls—which she'd been dying since the age of twenty-eight, a secret that she had made Kylie swear to never reveal that in public—and smiled. "I guess I held up just fine."

Ryan's eyes turned sullen. "I guess you did."

As Honey laid her arm across her grandson's shoulders in an effort to comfort him, Kylie bit back a sigh.

The video system and racing game had been a recent gift from NASCAR Sprint Cup Series driver Will Branch. Her job as a PR rep for Motor Media Group originally consisted of promoting Will, but now primarily involved keeping him out of trouble and, if he did get into trouble, getting him out with as much positive PR as possible.

Since Will's father, Hilton, who had disappeared in February after spending years bleeding the family coffers as well as their bank, was currently wanted by the feds *and* the subject of a just-released tell-all bestseller written by his long-time secret mistress, Will needed all the positive press he could get. This week had been particularly exhausting to both Will and Kylie as they tried to focus everyone on racing, not scandal.

So while she did her job and delivered good PR, her son got a three-hundred-dollar toy that she had to constantly monitor so he wouldn't flunk out of the fourth grade.

Fair, right?

And since Ryan and Will were about the same maturitywise, she couldn't even count him as a positive male adult role model. Which is what everybody constantly told her her son needed.

Ryan had her, a hip grandma, a beautiful home, decent grades, good friends and a passion and skill for playing for soccer.

A man who could never measure up to Matt was the last thing on his mind.

"Grab a water bottle and get in the truck," Kylie said, flexing her feet in her shoes and wishing she'd dashed upstairs to change instead of brooding.

"It's an *SUV,* Mom," Ryan shot back impatiently as he trotted from the room.

He'd corrected her four hundred times since she'd splurged on the brand new vehicle a month ago. The room inside allowed her to carry Ryan's soccer equipment and his boisterous friends. The big tires helped her go off-road at the race tracks she drove to—an important asset with the frequently gridlocked traffic. The size made her feel safe on the highway.

But anything with four-wheel drive was a *truck* in her book.

She started down the hallway to grab her wallet out of her briefcase, but Honey's words stopped her.

"The new soccer coach is very cute."

Kylie glanced at her mother over her shoulder, noting the shrewd twinkle in her eyes. "Oh, goody."

"He's an excellent coach, of course. Fun, but firm with the kids." Her smile widened. "And cute."

While her mother flitted from one distinguished sailing captain to another at the local yacht club, Kylie's love life was nonexistent. For the most part, she was okay with that, but her mother never stopped trying to change her mind—even though the dates she'd forced her into since Matt's death had been awkward and awful. "Is that why you gave me the guilt trip last night over not coming to the first three practices?"

Honey laid a perfectly manicured hand on her chest. "Would I do that?"

"In a heartbeat."

"Actually, he's way too young for you."

Good grief. At thirty-two, she wasn't exactly old herself. But then this was no doubt some kind of reverse psychology on her mother's part. "He is, huh?"

"Twenty-six is the buzz among the other soccer moms."

Okay, so *that* was *young*.

Honey grinned. "But I hear he has brothers. Several cute, Irish, older ones, in fact."

"*Mom…*"

"It doesn't hurt to be on the lookout."

With deliberate briskness, Kylie walked from the kitchen to the hall, coming back with her wallet in her hand and dark sunglasses on her face. She sashayed in one, smooth circle around her mother. "Really? I'll be sure to let you know if I spot somebody—for you."

KYLIE SAT in the bleachers with the other soccer parents as they watched their kids run back and forth along the length of the bright green field behind their local YMCA.

Despite her demanding job and crazy travel schedule to attend races out of town for more than thirty weekends a year, Kylie did her best to spend every moment possible with her son during the week. She'd missed the first three practices of the upcoming fall league because MMG had been planning media and sponsor events to prepare for the upcoming Chase for the Championship.

Will making the Chase was critical for both the competition aspect and sponsor dollars.

Sitting beside the other parents, most of whom Kylie already knew from past seasons, she noted they wore shorts and T-shirts in the late August heat. She felt sticky and out of place, very much aware that most of Ryan's teammates not only had two parents, but some had a mom who stayed home instead of one who worked the crazy hours she did.

"Okay, guys," the coach shouted, "let's run through that drill one more time, then we're done."

Though it bugged her to admit it, her mom was right. The coach was cute. Actually, more than cute. He was smokin' hot. She might be a widow, and her emotions about men still shaky and confused, but her eyes worked just fine.

When Coach Treadway released his team a few minutes later, and Kylie waited for Ryan to gather his gear and head toward her, she noticed several moms talking to the coach.

He laughed at something one of them said, and

his bright smile changed his face from merely handsome to glowing. He had short, light brown hair, kissed by the sun and tanned skin that reminded her of a swimmer. Or, given the impressive muscles and lean body exposed by his shorts and navy T-shirt, maybe a surfer. His jaw was strong, and he was tall. From this distance, she couldn't discern his eye color, but she easily noticed his shoulders were broad, his body lean, and firm-looking biceps extended through the sleeves of his navy T-shirt. He was tall, but then from her height of five foot four, most men seemed so.

I'm checking this guy out.

The bizarre thought pushed through her with a jolt that forced her to turn away. Her husband had been tall, dark and handsome. He'd been loving, honorable and supportive. And she was ashamed by the direction of her thoughts.

"Hey, you must be Ryan's mom," a deep voice said from beside her.

Feeling her face heat and praying it didn't show, Kylie turned and held out her hand. "Yes. Kylie Palmer."

He grasped her hand briefly and smiled that warm, amazing smile. "I'm Arthur Treadway. Coach, to most people."

She angled her head. "You don't like Arthur?"

"Not particularly, no."

"Family name?"

"My grandfather." He winced. "And it sounds like a grandfather name."

"Someday you might not think that's such a terrible thing."

"Yeah. Probably." He passed a soccer ball from one hand to another in a way that showed off his easy, natural coordination. "Family's big in my family."

"How's that?"

"Irish Catholic. I have four brothers, three sisters, seven uncles, seven aunts and more than forty cousins."

"That's big."

"To say the least."

Where had the league found this guy? she couldn't help but wonder. If he really was twenty-six, it seemed unlikely that he had a ten-year-old son on the team. "So, how many kids do you have?"

"None." He grinned. "Patrick is one of my older brother's kids. I'm pretty athletic and single, so I volunteered to help the team."

Uh-huh. Pretty athletic was a serious understatement. The guy looked like he could swim across the Atlantic with one hand tied behind his back. Slightly suspicious, she crossed her arms over her chest. And what single, gorgeous, young guy spent his spare time with ten-year-olds? "No kidding."

He shrugged. "My nephew begged me until I gave in. And my schedule's flexible. So, here I am."

Here you are, indeed. Gorgeous and smiling. Athletic and available.

Disturbed that her thoughts had again drifted from the coach-to-mom arena and into man-to-woman territory, she took a step backward. "Well, it was nice to meet you. I'm sure I'll be seeing you a lot this season."

"That'll be good."

Her smiled tightened. Good, how? Because he liked parental participation and support, or because she—

Wow, she was really losing it. Maybe she should accept the next date her mom pushed on her. Clearly, she needed an outlet for the weird, stomach-fluttering emotions that had suddenly invaded her body.

"Mom, we gotta help Coach clean up," Ryan said as he raced toward her with his friend Patrick at his heels.

"Oh, okay." Kylie glanced around and noticed that she, the coach, Ryan and Patrick were alone at the field. "We can do that, I guess."

"There's a dance thing at the yacht club," Patrick said.

As the boys rolled their eyes, Ryan added, "Everybody else ran out of here like dancing something's cool."

It was. Or could be. At least with the right partner. But then Kylie didn't have a partner.

The deep-seated ache of loss that never seemed to fade completely washed over her full force. Her mother had lost her husband after nearly forty years of marriage, and she'd moved on much easier than Kylie, who had only been married eight years. How was that possible? Why couldn't *she* move on? Was it because she'd lost her father and her husband within a few years of each other? What was wrong with her that made her cling so tightly to the past?

"So, we'll clean up," she said with forced brightness.

Between the four of them, they gathered the balls, cones and nets quickly. Kylie found a jacket that somebody had left behind and tossed it over her arm as they headed to the parking lot. The adults were silent while the boys were jabbering about the latest video game.

Once they'd stored the equipment in the back of the coach's old-style jeep—which was convertible and *ultracool*, according to the boys—Kylie gripped her keys in her palm and headed for her own truck. Escaping the odd chemistry between her and her son's coach was a serious priority. Her stomach still vibrated with the uncomfortable, unfamiliar tension.

Oh, but it's not unfamiliar. It's just been suppressed for a long, long time.

She ignored her conscience and approached her truck.

Naturally, that was the moment she noticed her truck was lurching oddly to one side. By the time she reached the driver's side door, she realized why.

She had a flat.

"Well, hell."

"What?" Coach asked as he moved in behind her.

She clamped her hand over her mouth and cast a worried look over her shoulder, hoping the boys hadn't heard her curse. Ryan already thought *hell* and *damn* weren't real curses, so she'd have an interesting time giving her "cursing is only an excuse for not expressing your feelings intelligently" speech if she was spouting those very words herself.

But, *damn it,* sometimes a situation just called for a choice word or two.

Coach laid his hand briefly on her shoulder. "I got it."

"No, I—" She started to spin toward him and tell him about AAA, but he was already heading toward the back of her truck.

"You got the full tire for the spare," he said as he wrangled the big tire out of the back with ease. "Smart."

"But I have—"

"Hey, Mom, wouldn't it be cool if Will's crew could come in and do their thing?" Ryan made the sound effects of an air gun as he gestured toward the tires. "They do four tires in, like, fourteen seconds. They could do this in…"

"Three point five seconds," Patrick said with a cocky smile.

"Your mom would be proud of those math skills," Coach said as he rolled the tire toward the front of the truck.

"I've got an A, you know," Patrick said.

Coach ruffled his hair as he passed by his nephew. "I heard."

Kylie hovered just behind him, following him and feeling the need to explain about the pit-stop statistics. "I work for a PR firm that specializes in racing. Ryan gets carried away sometimes."

"I'll bet."

Even though her feet throbbed in her pumps, guilt also coursed through her. He shouldn't be doing all the work. "I can get this," she said as she grabbed the tire and tugged. She wasn't helpless.

He glanced at her over his shoulder. "But I'm offering to help. Chivalrous, huh?"

"It's—" She backed away from the heat and welcome in his pale blue, almost silver eyes. She wished she hadn't noticed the color. In fact, when was the last time she noticed the color of a man's eyes?

Four years, five months and eighteen days ago.

"I appreciate the gesture," she said finally, stepping back further.

"No problem." He worked the jack handle/wrench around a lug nut and tugged.

Too late, she noticed a jagged edge of metal at the end of the handle. "Coach, don't—" She grabbed his hand, jerking it away, but she wasn't fast enough. His hand had already scraped over the edge.

Even as she wrapped her hand around his wrist, she closed her other hand over her cell phone, tucked in her pants pocket, and considered whether she should call 911. Blood dripped off his palm, and her heart jumped. "Oh, man. I'll get help. You'll be fine." That jagged metal had to have ripped a nasty slice across his hand.

She had to have a towel in the back. Or hand wipes. No, those would sting, and they needed to stop the bleeding ASAP. The first-aid kit. Hadn't Ryan's science teacher just given his students the speech about making sure their parents carried one in their car?

"Ryan, get the first-aid kit from the glove box,"

she said as she shoved her phone back in her pocket and yanked the hem of her shirt from her pants, wrapping the cloth around the coach's hand.

"What? Why?" Ryan, with Patrick at his heels, ground to a halt beside her and his coach. "Blood? Cool. Mom—"

"*Now*, Ryan."

"It's fine," Coach said, trying to pull his hand back as Ryan darted for the truck. "You're ruining your shirt."

She held tight, unbuttoning her shirt with her free hand, grateful she'd worn a tank top underneath. "I can get a new shirt."

"I'll pay for it."

"Whatever."

"I'm not usually so clumsy and stupid."

"Clumsy has nothing to do with—" She stopped as her gaze connected with his. A self-censure lurked in his eyes that seemed out of sync with a simple accident. "It'll be fine," she said calmly, softly.

The brief moment of vulnerability was gone. He flicked his gaze down. "Yeah."

"Kit," Ryan said as he appeared next to them and opened the plastic container.

Kylie pealed back her shirt a little to check the blood flow from his palm. It was already slowing, and the cut didn't seem as deep as she'd initially assumed. She let out the breath she'd been holding. "Open the big bandage and antibiotic ointment," she said to Ryan as she reapplied her shirt and the pressure.

"My mom faints at the sight of blood," Patrick said, leaning close to study his uncle's hand.

"She does?" Kylie asked. How had the woman made it ten years with a son? Kylie had patched up road rash, cuts, removed dozens of splinters and all but performed major surgery on Ryan since the moment he'd figured out how to crawl.

Coach shook his head at Patrick. An unspoken message passed between them.

"Well, sorta," Patrick amended. "It was just that one time."

Ryan looked as if he wanted to press for more details for a second, but he obviously thought better of it since he held the big bandage by the corners and said nothing else.

Kylie, who had plenty of emotions and private thoughts, certainly had no plans to ask about the Treadway family. Between her and Ryan, they managed to apply the ointment and bandage to Coach's hand with all the efficiency of a nurse and her assistant.

"Thanks. You guys are quite a team," he said, flexing his fingers. "But we still have a flat to deal with."

"I got it," Kylie said, moving toward the truck.

He grabbed her arm. "I'll do it."

Kylie narrowed her eyes. Was this some kind of macho guy thing?

"Ah, Coach," Ryan began a bit nervously, "my mom can do it. Patrick and I can help. You're, you know…hurt."

Steely determination slid into Coach's eyes. "I'm fine."

Ryan's gaze darted from his coach to his mom. "Okay."

"Why don't you boys work on your passing for a minute while I talk with Coach?" Kylie said, careful to keep her voice calm and even. Once the boys scooted off, Kylie leveled the full force of her tremble-in-the-shoes glare at Ryan's coach. "The boys are gone. Your macho coach rep is safe. Your hand has to be throbbing like crazy. How about you take some Tylenol and sit down?"

He crossed his arms over his impressively broad chest. "No."

Kylie suppressed an eye roll and opened the driver's door. She tossed her ruined shirt on the seat, then retrieved a towel that she wrapped around the jagged edge of the wrench. "Fine by me." She hooked the wrench around the lug nut and tugged. It barely budged.

How many times had she seen NASCAR teams perform this deal? And with considerably more grace, though also with significantly more muscle.

Where was an air gun and seven over-the-wall guys when a girl needed them?

"You want some help?" Coach asked from behind her.

She gritted her teeth and tugged again. "No."

"Sure?"

Sweat rolled down her spine as she managed to loosen one lug nut and move on to the second. "Yes."

After she'd managed to loosen the second one—though it seemed to take hours—he had the nerve to say, "I could do it one-handed."

She glared at him over her shoulder. "Is that supposed to be encouraging?"

"I guess not."

"Then shut up."

She wrangled with the third lug nut. Her arms ached, and the sense of pride she'd started with was fading fast. She wasn't some helpless girly-girl who fainted over the sight of blood and needed a man to bail her out of every tight spot. She could do this.

"We could work as a team," Coach suggested.

Tired, sweaty and embarrassed, she slumped. "I guess we could."

Without further comment, he added his muscle to her efforts and they managed to change the tire quickly.

"It's not my rep with the boys that I'm worried about," he said as he helped her tighten the last lug nut.

"No?" she asked absently, staring at the tire to admire their efforts. She'd done it. Well, they had. No wonder there were guys lined up around the block to be part of the over-the-wall crew in racing.

"I'd just rather not look like an idiot in front of a beautiful woman."

She jerked her head around and stared at him. "Who?"

He tapped her nose with the tip of his finger. "You, of course."

Was he *flirting* with her?

No.

Maybe?

She swallowed. Even if flirting were remotely possible, this guy was way too young for her to consider being picked up by. Hunky and charming, definitely. But young.

Nerves fluttered in her stomach. Because of the awkwardness of the situation, of course. She'd practically given him the shirt off her back, then there was that flash of emotion she suspected he wouldn't normally let anyone see. She felt as though she knew something personal about him now, and that knowledge changed him from the cute soccer coach to…well, more.

But there wasn't more.

Right?

"I—" Wow, it had been a long time since she'd talked to a man without the added baggage of motherhood and widowhood. She'd probably forgotten how. "I don't think you're an idiot."

"Good. I don't think you're a feminist control freak."

She started to be offended, but who could be angry in the face of that charming smile? "I guess we're even."

He flexed the fingers of his left hand, covered in the bandage she'd applied. "Thanks, by the way."

She held up the towel-wrapped wrench. "You're welcome, and I'm sorry you were hurt. I'll call the dealer tomorrow and complain."

He held out his uninjured hand, which she took,

and he helped her stand. "Beautiful women who save my life get to call me Sean."

"I didn't really save—" She stopped and stared at him. "Why would they call you Sean?"

"It's my middle name. My close friends and family call me that, because it's less confusing around my grandfather."

"Whose name is Arthur."

"Right."

"So most people call you Coach, your close friends and family call you Sean. Who calls you Arthur?"

"Business associates."

"Oh-kay." That was a few too many names if you asked her, but she supposed everybody had their issues. And Sean did suit him better—traditionally Irish, but also modern and strong.

"You're pretty handy to have around in a crisis," Coach, ah...*Sean* said. "You didn't panic and moved quickly."

"It's part of my job. I'm efficient."

He paused, his gaze roving over her face. "I bet you're a whole lot more."

CHAPTER TWO

TURNING AWAY from Kylie's puzzled expression and his own odd feelings, Sean gave his attention to the boys. "How about pizza?"

The boys, who'd seemed completely engrossed in passing a soccer ball back and forth until that moment, dashed toward him. "All right!"

Kylie shook her head. "Oh, I don't—"

"Come on." Sean grinned. "Unless you're planning to dance—" he mimicked a couple twirling "—the night away."

"Me? No, I don't have—" She paused, her expression darkening. "I'm not going to the yacht club."

The change from beautiful and confident to sad and embarrassed made him want to bring her smile back. "Good, then you're ready for the best pizza on the lake."

"I have some work…" She glanced down at her son, who was giving her his best pleading look. After a moment, she sighed and slid her fingers through Ryan's hair. "Okay. Pizza it is."

While the boys cheered, Kylie turned toward

Sean. "I just need to call my mother and tell her we're not coming home right away."

He lifted his eyebrows. "You live with your mother?"

She sank her teeth into her bottom lip. "It's the wild and crazy widowed life."

Distracted by her lush, pink lips, Sean had to drag his gaze away. But his view merely landed on her deep blue eyes, which were equally engrossing. Sadness lingered in them, an emotion he both understood and felt compelled to conquer.

"Ryan told me his father was a policeman and that he died in the line of duty," he said quietly. "I'm sorry."

"Thanks. My mom's support helps." She held up her cell phone. "Who I need to call. After I talk to her, I'll follow you to the pizza place."

She was dismissing the topic of past—and maybe present—hurts. He understood the need for discretion and privacy well. "Sounds good."

"I wanna ride with Coach," Ryan said. "Okay, Mom?"

"As long as it's okay with him."

"Fine by me. Just make sure you signal if the tire does anything weird."

"Will do."

Sean walked to his jeep, then loaded the boys and made sure they had their seat belts fastened before pulling out of the parking lot and heading to Mario's.

Just as his family was large and Irish Catholic, Mario's was large and Italian Catholic. They'd bonded after Sean had moved from his family's South Carolina farm to the Charlotte area a few years ago to join his older brothers' security firm, and Mario had moved from New York to make his distinct stamp on the culinary world.

Without significant cash flow, Mario's start was a strip mall pizza joint, but Sean had no doubt his friend would find his four stars eventually. Mario had the whole package—family secret marinara sauce, handmade pizza dough and pasta, an amazing touch with spices and a work ethic that never rested. For a bachelor, the restaurant was nirvana, and as a friend, Mario was the best.

After Kylie parked her SUV next to his in the parking lot, their group walked into the restaurant. Being a weeknight, the diners were somewhat scarce. Striding toward a vacant table, Sean caught Mario's gaze via the open-air kitchen. "Sausage and pepperoni?" Mario called.

Sean pointed to Kylie and the boys. "We'll see."

His friend's dark eyebrows rose as his gaze slid to Kylie. He gave Sean a grin and a thumbs-up.

They gathered in a red vinyl-cushioned booth and argued lightly about what to get. The boys wanted the meat and cheese overload, and Kylie tried to push broccoli and pineapple.

"Broccoli *and* pineapple?" Sean asked.

"A vegetable and a fruit," she said, looking at him head-on as if daring him to dispute her choice.

"Guys need protein," he said.

"*Everybody* needs protein. Gallons of saturated fat aren't so desirable, however."

From the other side of the table, the boys silently watched their exchange.

"Is this a mom thing?" he asked them.

"Yep," they answered together.

Laying one arm along the back of the booth, Sean angled his body toward Kylie. He felt slightly out of his element, but it certainly wasn't the first time. "I'll bet most days you go for the low-fat, heavy-on-the-vegetables, sensible meal."

She narrowed her eyes. "Is that a dig?"

"No way. My sisters-in-law do the same." He winked. "Have to worry about those ten-year-old arteries, don't we?"

"Okay, I *know* that was a dig."

Grinning, he leaned forward. "Maybe just a small one. But Ryan eats so good the rest of the week, don't you think one indulgence would be okay?"

"Are your game day strategies this obvious?"

The boys laughed.

Sean sat back.

Since he appeared to be on his own, he scrambled to remember the moves he used to finesse his own mom. Thankfully, he recalled the delicate art of compromise. "How about one vegetarian, and one double-meat?"

"As long as we order a big salad first," she said after a long pause.

"Deal!" the boys said before Sean could respond.

After they ordered, Sean explained how he knew Mario, and assured them his friend made the best pizza in the world. The boys could only sit still for grown-up talk for a few minutes, though, and begged for money for the game room. Apparently figuring she'd scored her mom points for the day by making them eat salad, Kylie dug out quarters, then sent the boys to the small room across the restaurant where all the other kids had gathered.

Alone with Kylie, Sean reflected on the moment she'd stepped onto his practice field. Elegant in her office attire when nearly everybody else wore shorts and T-shirts, she'd stood out instantly. In just the last hour, he'd also learned she was kind but firm with Ryan. She was beautiful, smart, witty and resourceful.

Even with the *STAY BACK!* vibes he got from her, he couldn't deny his interest in finding out more. Still, a widow with a young son carried a lot of baggage. She was the mother of one of his players. Plus, she had a connection to him—and his job—he didn't exactly want to advertise.

"So," she said, hitting him with her laser blue gaze, "you said earlier your schedule is flexible. What do you do?"

"I work with my older brothers. They have a security firm."

Her face paled. "Security?"

"Mostly systems installations."

For them, though, not me.

He justified the half truth by reminding himself her police officer husband had died in the line of duty. The last thing she needed to hear from him was that his job wasn't a whole lot safer.

Plus, he simply didn't talk about his work with anybody.

Secrets were required, not convenient.

"And you work in racing PR," he said.

She sipped her soda. "My primary responsibility is NASCAR driver Will Branch."

"So Ryan told me."

She shifted uncomfortably. "He brags sometimes."

"It's a way to one-up your friends when your goal kicks are a bit weak."

"Ryan's goal kicks are weak?"

"A little. He just needs more practice. His ball-handling skills are primo, though, so he's doing great there. He'll grow into his muscles, and I could show him some strengthening exercises that might help the kicks."

She bit her lip, distracting him from the soccer topic. "That would be good, but he wants to be perfect." When he didn't answer, she continued, "How do I fight that?"

He dragged his gaze from her lush mouth. "Remind him that his personal best is all that's important."

"Oh, yeah. That'll be easy. He and Patrick compete like it's the last lap at Daytona every day."

"It's a man thing."

Her lips turned up. "And a thing Mom can't grasp."

He grinned. "Not if she's too focused on fruits and vegetables."

"No wonder you're such a good coach. You're just like them."

He looked over her face and down her body. "I'm no ten-year-old boy."

Her gaze flicked to his and held. "No," she said slowly. "No, you certainly aren't."

"Mom, we need more quarters," Ryan said as he and Patrick appeared next to the table.

"I got it," Sean said, sliding out of the booth and heading toward his jeep. He gathered all the coins he could from his console, then walked back to the table. After handing the boys more money, he settled into the booth again, noticing that though Kylie had inched backward to the far corner of the bench seat, her face was still flushed.

Was it possible his curiosity and attraction wasn't one-sided?

"How do you like coaching so far?" she asked before he could direct the conversation to a more personal topic.

"It's great. I'm not so old that I don't remember what it's like to be ten, full of energy, skinny and awkward."

"I can't imagine you feeling awkward, and you're certainly not old."

"Same goes."

She shook her head. "Maybe I'm past awkward, and I'm not *old*, but I'm older than you." Her gaze flicked to his. Hesitation, but unmistakable heat lingered in her eyes. "Not a big feat, I guess."

"Older than me?" He leaned toward her, liking the

way her eyes widened. "Really? How do you know that?"

"I heard you—" She bit her lip again.

Mentally groaning—the woman knew how to torture lips and men—he somehow managed to say, "I never would have figured you for somebody who followed gossip."

She raised her eyebrows, the momentary uncertainty in her expression gone. "I don't."

"Good for you. Me, either."

She was such a dichotomy. Confident and uncertain. Shy and bold. Where was the real Kylie? And why did he want so badly to find her?

He let his gaze travel over her lovely face. "I prefer to find out my information firsthand."

"Me, too." She met his gaze head-on. "I heard you were twenty-six and single. True?"

"Yes."

"And that you were cute, Irish and had several older brothers."

"Two older, two younger." He grinned. "And you'll have to take my mother's word about the cute part."

"Since *my* mother made that observation, I guess I'll have to bow to the authorities."

"A wise move. What else?"

She sipped her soda. "What else what?"

"About me."

"Oh." She shrugged. "That's it."

"*That's it?* You weren't more curious?"

"No."

Annoyed, he drummed his fingers on the table. "My older brothers are married, and my younger ones are still in college."

"No kidding?"

"*I'm* the single, available one."

"I'll alert all my single, available friends."

"You're single."

"I'm widowed."

"And not available?"

"I—" She glanced down, then back at him. "I'm certainly not widowed and desperate."

"You think I'm only interested in widowed and desperate women?"

She angled her head. "I'm sure you could have your pick of anybody."

Maybe he could.

Maybe, when he and Mario went out to the local bars and nightclubs, they never spent much time alone. Maybe he'd enjoyed his players' moms matchmaking and attention. Maybe the women in his past who'd learned what he did for a living had flushed with excitement and imagined danger and glamour, and maybe he'd used that to his advantage.

But when he'd seen Kylie, something inside him had clicked. And he wanted to find out what.

"You're my son's soccer coach," she said when he remained silent.

"You want to leave it at that?"

Before she could answer, the pizza arrived, and the boys rushed back to the table seconds later. The tension between him and Kylie dissipated, forcing him to set aside personal issues and join the world of ten-year-old boys.

As always, Patrick and Ryan's energy and enthusiasm made him smile. Their world was so small, wide-eyed and promising. Though Ryan's father's death had no doubt caused him incredible pain and changed him forever, he was young enough—and had a strong enough support system—to still be full of hope and move on with his life.

Kylie's pain wasn't so easy to escape. Did she still miss her husband, or did she simply hold herself back so she wouldn't have to suffer again? He sensed a need for her to step outside her comfort zone, yet she couldn't fully open the door. She stood behind a screen, sensing something great might be out there, but too wary to move toward it.

It was probably better if they kept their attraction buried. It would complicate both their lives.

But then he'd never been afraid of complications before. And while he considered the risks he took with his job calculated ones, many people would say he wasn't at all careful, that he enjoyed danger.

And maybe he did.

Later, as they walked to their respective cars, his phone beeped. He checked the screen to find a message from his brother Jeremy. *Got a lead on Branch.*

His heartbeat accelerated; his blood heated. The thrill of the chase. Would he ever tire of that special form of edgy excitement?

"Got a hot chick on the line?" Kylie asked when he flipped the phone closed.

He glanced at her—and his heart rate sped up for an entirely different reason. "No. Duty calls."

She glanced at her watch. "It's nearly nine o'clock."

"My hours are flexible but long."

Shrugging, she opened the door to her SUV. "Well, thanks for dinner. We'll return the favor sometime."

"Yeah?" He leaned close and whispered, "How about Friday night? Just you and me this time."

She shifted her gaze to her son, who was talking to Patrick and ignoring them, then shook her head. "I'm off to Bristol. Press interviews and qualifying in the afternoon, then back for a meeting with an associate sponsor."

"Saturday night?"

"I go back to Bristol Saturday morning and stay until Sunday night."

He frowned. "Are you *ever* free on the weekend?"

"From Thanksgiving to New Year's. And I thought we'd decided you're my son's soccer coach."

"I am. But I don't see what that has to do with us."

She met his gaze directly. "I'm flattered, Sean. Really. But I'm not available for a just-you-and-me dinner."

"Yeah." He stepped back. "Okay. I guess I'll see you at practice."

"Sure." She climbed into her SUV, then drove off seconds later.

As he watched her go, disappointment settled heavily into his chest. He wanted—badly—to see her again. In fact, he wanted to know everything about her.

SEAN LEANED BACK in his office chair and closed his eyes as he sipped his second cup of morning coffee. Any minute now the caffeine was going to kick in, and he'd have the energy to do something besides imagine the curvy body, smile and full, pink lips of one Kylie Palmer.

Given the perfection of her lips, though, he suspected he could happily fantasize for days.

"How did the stakeout go?" Jeremy asked abruptly from the doorway.

Only years of experience and training kept Sean from wincing with guilt. He hadn't remotely considered any aspect of the stakeout in hours.

He didn't open his eyes as he responded. "Long, boring and unproductive."

"That was a good tip. Bart Branch *was* at the charity event, wasn't he?"

"He was there." He frowned. "At least I think it was Bart. Him and Will are identical down to the last damn freckle. I wonder if they ever switch race cars on the NASCAR officials, just to shake things up." He waved the passing idea aside. "Anyway, I doubt even his own father could have gotten within fifty feet of him. The Harmon Tools Girls pretty much had him covered."

"The Harmon Tools Girls?"

They gave him the energy to smile. "One of his secondary sponsor's idea of eye candy. Pretty good idea, actually," he added, remembering the girls who fawned over Bart Branch and his fellow NASCAR drivers and no doubt sold quite a few hammers and drill bits in the process. "They have their own tool belts." He opened his eyes and met his brother's gaze. "And *very* short shorts."

Jeremy settled into the single chair in front of Sean's cluttered, battered desk. "So no sign of Hilton Branch?"

"It was a long shot that he'd risk such a public event—even to see one of his kids."

"We gotta check out every possibility."

"True. But Daddy Branch and his millions of absconded bank funds are still in the wind."

"Along with our lucrative bounty."

"I'll find him." Sean sipped from his mug. "After another gallon or two of this stuff."

Jeremy speared his hand through his hair. "We need that bounty."

"I know what's at stake."

"You don't have a wife and kids to support."

"But I have you to nag me instead. Where's a good woman when you need one?"

"Speaking of a woman…are you going to tell me about pizza with Will Branch's PR rep?"

He stiffened. While he'd known for weeks what Kylie did, and he'd considered the possibility of garnering information through that connection. But that was no longer possible. Before, Kylie Palmer was the mother of one of his soccer kids. She was just another person who worked in the NASCAR world, the world he had to penetrate and investigate in order to accomplish his assignment.

But how could he let Kylie, the lovely, pink-lipped object of his fantasies, be simply a tool for his job?

"I guess Patrick told you about last night," he said finally.

Jeremy nodded.

And knowing his brother's thoroughness with research, he undoubtedly had a file on Kylie. The existence of—and his access to—that file made Sean uncomfortable, almost as much as it roused his curiosity. He'd told her he liked to find out about people from the source, not gossip. Was he now prepared to pretend he hadn't said those words merely to get a deeper glimpse into her life?

Was it possible to get to know her and still responsibly handle his case? He and his brothers had been hired to find Will Branch's father, to bring him before the court to face justice for stealing millions in bank funds. He'd stripped his family of their support and dignity and left his twin sons without racing sponsors.

His family and the bank executives were furious with him, the FBI wanted him in cuffs and the SEC was chomping at the bit to talk to him, but Sean knew *he'd* be the one to find him. He hadn't failed yet, and he had no intention of ruining his record.

But he couldn't use Kylie to accomplish his goal. He wouldn't add to her pain and sense of betrayal. He'd watched her tousle her son's hair, and he'd fantasized about her lips. There was no going back to being casual acquaintances. He *knew* her. And wanted to know more.

Still, the danger, the *temptation*, to tune his ears and pick up on any bit of information, no matter how inadvertent or innocent, lay next to him like a coiled snake.

"She might know something," Jeremy said into the charged silence.

Sean set aside his coffee and stood, turning away. "She doesn't," he said with more hope than assurance.

Jeremy sighed. "A widow with a son? Not your usual type."

"Things change."

"I've never questioned your tactics in getting a job done."

"So don't start now."

"The balloon payment on this place is due in a month, and we're short. We have to have that bounty."

Sean stared at an ancient oak through the back window of the renovated house where he and his brothers had moved their offices from a dingy strip mall two years ago. The location in the suburbs of Charlotte had been the perfect place to base their more secretive operations, which he oversaw, while building a lucrative income on the security systems installations his brothers handled. "We'll make the payment."

"I'm counting on you."

Sean turned to smile at his brother. "Consider it done."

CHAPTER THREE

"HE SENT ME a brand-new shirt. Plus, he didn't ask for tickets or pit passes," Kylie said, stirring her margarita. "Not even an autograph."

Her closest friend, Felicia, licked salt off the tip of her finger. "The creep."

"Don't you think that's suspicious?"

"It's criminal."

"You think I'm making too much of this."

Felicia widened her golden-brown eyes in horror. "Oh, no. I think we should lock him up and throw away the key." She paused and grinned, flicking her long blond hair over her shoulder. "As long as I get the key and the exclusive right to interrogate the super sexy soccer coach under hot lights for hours on end."

"You're not funny. This is serious."

"No, this is a sign from the heavens. It's about time you started dating again."

Kylie choked. She was absolutely *not* dating Sean. Or anybody else. "I'm not—"

"Ready? Yeah, yeah, blah, blah. Come on, Kylie. You have a caution sign tattooed on your forehead.

Do you know how embarrassing that is for a woman in my position?"

"In *your* position?"

Felicia sighed. "*Hellooo?* Wedding planner. I can't have unhappy, single friends. It's like false advertising."

"I'm not single. I'm a widow."

"And it's past time you take another chance on love."

"No."

"You can't bury yourself with Matt."

Kylie flinched and was suddenly very sorry she'd let her friend talk her into a drink after work.

Felicia laid her hand briefly over Kylie's. "I'm sorry. That came out lousy. Matt was the greatest. Didn't I plan your wedding? Didn't I tell you he was the man who'd make you happy?"

"Happy forever, you said." Kylie shook her head. "It didn't last forever."

"It would have. It *should* have." She paused, her eyes darkening with sadness and regret. "It just didn't."

"And I should be over it by now," Kylie said, knowing she sounded defensive and unreasonable.

"No. You'll never be completely over Matt. You shouldn't be. And you've got a son who'll always be a daily reminder of the love you guys shared. But you do need to move on."

Kylie studied her friend, and, for the first time, actually listened. "So you've been saying."

"For a couple of years now." Felicia dipped a corn chip in salsa. "Ever since Ryan's cute second grade teacher gave you his special smile in the carpool line."

"Some love life manager you are. That guy worked his way through every single mom with a kid in his or anybody else's second grade class."

"I never said he was loyal, just cute." She sipped her margarita. "And we were talking about the sexy soccer coach."

Kylie drummed her fingers on the table. He was sexy. *Young* and sexy. But, in looking back at last night, she'd been unusually dazzled. Now, she was suspicious of him and his charming smile. "Who doesn't ask for autographs?"

Felicia shrugged. "Maybe he doesn't like racing."

"Even people who don't like racing know about Will and his family scandal. Plus, people get drivers' autographs and sell them on ebay all the time. It's practically a cottage industry."

Felicia's eyes twinkled with excitement. "Maybe— and here's a *really* wild thought—he's not interested in anything but you."

"Yeah, right. He's twenty-six."

"Mmm. Younger men have so much…energy."

"Be serious."

"Nah. I'd rather hear about Coach Treadway."

Knowing Felicia was one of the few people she could share her embarrassing attraction to her son's coach, Kylie took a bracing sip of her drink, then admitted, "He asked me to call him Sean."

"What did you expect to call him? *Coach*?"

"That's probably better." Certainly less…intimate.

"It's his middle name. Only his family and close friends call him that. I'm not family or a close friend."

"Oh, but you could be so much more." Eyes sparkling, Felicia leaned forward. "Just how gorgeous is he?"

"Pretty gorgeous. I keep having this image of him surfing or laying that incredible body on an exotic beach somewhere."

Felicia expelled a sigh of bliss. "A free spirit. A great opposite for you."

"I'm not *that* intense." Kylie played with the stem of her glass. Ryan and her mother both often accused her of being too forceful and controlling. "I can be flexible."

"Uh, I don't think so, girl. I'm the one who took that yoga class with you, remember?" They both burst out laughing at the memory of how bad she was.

Self-evaluation was a pain in the butt. Still, Kylie realized her sense of protection and fear often stood in her way. Part of her knew it was time to stop living in the past. Part of her knew she had to at least *consider* dating again. Part of her didn't want to be alone forever.

The rest of her, however, was scared to the bone.

"Even Matt would think you're stuck in a rut," Felicia said.

Kylie raised her eyebrows. "Now you're the conscience of my dead husband?"

"I'm your best friend, which means I'm in charge of kicking your butt when necessary."

"Humph." Kylie could feel her lip moving into a

pout, so she immediately scowled. "So I'll be friendly with the cute soccer coach."

Felicia's determined gaze didn't budge.

"And I'll consider accepting a date."

"When?"

"Soon."

Felicia toasted her. "I'm holding you to it."

"Yeah, yeah." Digging into the chips and looking for a way to shift the spotlight away from her, Kylie tried to remember what was going on in Felicia's life at the moment. "How's the Marlowe wedding coming?"

"Slowly. And cheaply. The bride's father actually insisted I go to his restaurant supplier and rent glassware."

"Don't people *usually* rent glasses for a reception?"

"Not from Economy Is Us. I mean, *really*. Can you imagine a guest complimenting your dream wedding decor and you saying 'Oh, yes, isn't it lovely? We had it all done through *Economy Is Us*?'"

As Kylie stifled a laugh, Felicia shuddered. "It's insane. They're a cut-rate supplier and wouldn't know decent crystal if it danced a jig in front of their faces." Clearly disgusted, Felicia sighed. "The wedding is three weeks away! They're lucky vendors are even *entertaining* the idea of changes at this point. Plus, if the father of the bride owns Marlowe Communications and is worth eighty million dollars, he should *at least* spring for top-flight designer glassware for the head table. It's *humiliating*."

"The cheapness of the human race is appalling."

Gesturing with a salsa-covered chip, Felicia narrowed her eyes. "A sneering comment from a woman who works in an industry that pays thousands for a set of tires is wholly without credibility."

Kylie laughed. "Point made."

"If only your mother would remarry. Talk about class."

Kylie shook her head. "She's having too much fun moving from captain to captain."

"*Captain.* Like these guys command *The Queen Mary.*"

"Around here they think they do."

"I could handle the egos if I had the right budget."

"Come to the track with me sometime and network. Lots of potential, moneyed grooms in racing."

Felicia wrinkled her nose. "Do you know anybody with a suite, or do I have to hang around in the infield?"

"How about infield before the race, then a suite during?"

"Deal. I'll let you know when I have a free weekend."

"You really need to get over the noise thing, you know. You listen to future in-laws shouting at each other every other week. Revving engines are exciting, not annoying."

"Exciting to you, maybe. And the in-laws I can handle. It's the shrieking brides that make my ears ring."

By the time Kylie and Felicia finished their drinks and caught up on what was going on with mutual friends, it was eight o'clock. With guilt riding her, Kylie strode briskly into her mom's house, trying to remember if she'd bought all Ryan's school supplies. Where had the summer gone? After beach trips, sleepovers and weekends at the race track, she had no idea how she'd get him back into academic mode.

She found him and Honey in the media room, engrossed in another intense match of video game racing.

"I need more room in Turn Two," Ryan said.

"Too bad, kiddo," Honey said, her eyes intently focused on the TV screen.

Her car—obviously the purple and pink one—slid by Ryan's on the inside as if he was standing still. She crowded him, but passed him clean.

Much to her son's frustration.

It had to be tough on a ten-year-old ego to have your sixty-plus grandma outracing you. But then Honey had an abundance of nerves of steel.

How had those genes gone so awry in Kylie? Why, at least in her personal life, did she pull back more often than she pushed forward? Why did she always err on the side of caution? Was that why she enjoyed racing so much, because it was wild and on the edge, something she could never be?

Why couldn't she return Sean's flirting? Why did he intimidate her so thoroughly?

Technically, she was single. Matt would never begrudge her moving her on with her life. He'd want her to be happy. Felicia and her mother thought she was in a rut. Even Ryan, as much as he'd idolized his father, asked her a few weeks ago why she didn't have a boyfriend like their divorced neighbor, Mrs.—now Ms.—Bailey.

Leaning against the doorframe of the media room, unnoticed by her mother and son, Kylie couldn't admit to any of them the real problem—she was happier living in the past.

She and Matt had been married for eight years. Eight Christmases, birthdays and anniversaries. Shared friends and colleagues. He'd worked security at the track when the NASCAR races were held in town. He'd shared joys and burdens, organizing play dates and staying up through the night, comforting Ryan through colic and colds.

And he'd served his community and his family selflessly, right up until the moment he'd died instantly and violently at the hands of a convenience store robber with a stolen pistol.

She'd had little choice but to accept his fate and hers, even when the memories grabbed her by her throat, robbing her of coherent thought, and she cried in the dark and pretended to be strong. Now, out of self-protection, she thought of Matt and their life in a dreamlike way, almost as if it had never happened.

If not for their son, she might have even been able to believe that for more than a few moments.

Still, beyond the pain, anger and frustration, there was something in Sean's eyes that had sparked an interest she'd kept dormant for four long years. Was she brave enough, smart enough, crazy enough to see where that led? Or would she crawl back into her shell, to the comfortable—if cowardly—past where she'd been hiding?

Knowing she was on the verge of sinking into self-pity mode, she moved into the room where Ryan and her mother were playing their game. "Is there a caution lap in the near future?"

Shoulders hunched over their identical mini steering wheels both simply grunted and never took their eyes off the TV screen.

Kylie figured she'd been demoted to kitchen duty.

She headed downstairs and cleaned the remains of dinner, then reheated the chicken casserole and vegetables her mother had set aside for her. She ate on the screened porch, watching the lake water ripple and the skyline streak in orange and pink.

Though she'd been through plenty of pain in her life, she was lucky. She was amazingly grateful for her mother, who was on hand to make dinner and take care of Ryan when Kylie had to work or wanted to meet a friend for a drink. Her mother would certainly rather her go on a date than hang out with Felicia, but she was a rock of support—both emotional and financial—that so many single moms had no access to.

Kylie had a great kid. Hard to handle and overly energetic at times, but she'd worry more if he sat around all day like a lump. He was bright and kind. A good friend and a good sport.

Yeah, she was lucky.

"You okay?"

Kylie smiled over her shoulder as Honey walked onto the porch. "I'm great. How'd the race go?"

"I won." She sank into the wicker chair next to Kylie's. "I advised your son to hit the showers and cool off."

"*My* son, huh?"

"He didn't get that competitive streak from me."

"Oh, you're not serious. Where do you think he got it?"

Pursing her lips, Honey tucked her hair behind her ear. "I have no idea."

Kylie smiled and leaned her head back against the chair.

"I'm proud of you," Honey said.

"Yeah?"

"Yeah. I know I harp on you about working too many hours and not dating enough, but you're doing pretty great. You—we—are making a good life for Ryan." She reached over and grasped her hand, giving it a light squeeze. "Two old widows, raising a son."

"Old?" Thinking of young, hard-bodied and beautiful Sean Treadway, Kylie winced. "We're not old. We're—"

Ryan stormed onto the porch. "Mom! Why do you have to work so much?"

So much for peace. "I have to do my job. I took off early yesterday, if you remember."

"Do you have to work all weekend?" he asked accusingly.

"You know I do," Kylie returned calmly, though her stomach tightened with guilt.

"I hate your work."

"I'm sorry you do. I like it very much."

"I hate—"

"Don't disrespect your mother," Honey said with a pointed glare in her grandson's direction.

Ryan crossed his arms over his chest. "And why do *you* have to win my games all the time?"

Realizing his frustration with the game was at the root of his anger, Kylie let her own anxiety go. Raising kids was a wild, shaky minefield. "Why don't you invite a friend to hang out with you Friday at Bristol?" she suggested to Ryan. Though it was a three hour drive, she and Ryan were going up for qualifying and the scheduled press interviews, then they had to come back that night so she could attend the sponsor meeting in Charlotte Saturday morning. "Honey can go with us and look out for you when I'm working."

Ryan's gaze cut toward hers. His gaze was speculative. "Can I go into one of the suites?"

"We'll see."

"Can I hang out in Will's pit box?"

"If you stay out of the way."

"Can I go into the hauler?"

"Maybe on qualifying day. It's less hectic."

"And an adult has to be with you at all times," Honey pointed out with a resigned look in her eyes, probably realizing she'd be the adult in question.

Ryan smiled. "Cool. I want to invite Coach Treadway."

CHAPTER FOUR

Hi, Coach…um, Sean. This is Kylie Palmer, Ryan's mother…

Sean fantasized about Kylie's enticing lips as he listened to his cell phone voice mail for probably the tenth time.

"Ryan would, ah…like to invite you to the track at Bristol with him this Friday," Kylie continued. "I usually let him invite a friend…a friend his own age most of the time, but he's insisting…he would really like you to come. I'll be working, but available by cell phone. I—" She stopped, sighing audibly. "I know it's a lot to ask. If you could get back to me as soon as possible, I'd appreciate it."

Once again pressing the Save button, Sean leaned back in his desk chair. He liked the way her voice was hesitant at first, then became brisk, professional, almost distant as she explained that her *son* wanted him to spend Friday with him, but *she* had no interest in him whatsoever. Then she softened, the longing to make Ryan happy evident.

If he could direct that longing in another direction…

He'd spent most of the night trolling the Charlotte

airport, on yet another dead end tip of Hilton Branch's whereabouts. A business associate of Branch's had been certain he'd attempt to come to Charlotte to see his sons. After checking dozens of flights, charming dozens of airline employees and slipping cash to several baggage handlers, he'd come up empty on leads and exhausted himself to the point that he'd barely dragged himself out of bed at noon.

Oh, yeah, you're a great dating candidate for a single mom.

Still, he dialed her number.

"Kylie Palmer."

"Hi, Kylie. It's Sean."

"Hi. I...I guess you got my message."

"I did. I'd love to come to Bristol with Ryan on Friday."

"Okay." She cleared her throat. "I'll put through a rush on credentials for you. I'll need your driver's license number."

He gave her the information. A background check, no doubt, making sure he wasn't an escape felon. How ironic. "What time should I pick you guys up?"

"Ah...actually we'll be picking you up." she said. "I have to have my car in case there's an emergency."

"Like a medical emergency?"

"Like a beer and snack emergency."

"For who?"

"That was a very inappropriate thing for me to say," she muttered.

His smile widened. She was sharing. Reluctantly,

but the instinct was there. "Ryan and I just need a soda every couple of hours. Okay, maybe one an hour for him. Who's the beer for?"

"Nobody."

"The drivers?"

"No. They don't— Well, they do, just not during—" She sighed. "Of course none of the drivers drink beer during or before competition, but Friday is one of Will's buddy's birthday, so—"

"They're going to party like crazy."

She cleared her throat again. "I imagine so."

"Especially Will Branch," he couldn't help but add, though he questioned whether he was probing simply about her dealings with him, or for his own, case-sensitive information.

"I misspoke," Kylie said tightly. "Will Branch is an excellent driver and is proud to represent First Rate Auto Loans in the NASCAR Sprint Cup Series."

Sean said nothing for a moment, realizing he'd stepped over a line. "I'm not interviewing you. Or him."

"I know. My job's still the same."

And here he'd been worried about getting information from her and that he might have to consider whether or not to use it for his case. No worries there. The woman was an absolute clam.

"But I make you nervous."

"I'm not nervous."

"You sure?" he asked, wishing he could see her face. Was she flushed?

Happily or uncomfortably?

"Absolutely," she said.

In the end, he agreed to drive out to her mother's house on the lake and meet her. They'd leave from there to pick up Ryan from daycamp before heading to Bristol. As a date, it lacked romance and intimacy—face it, he was pretty much the babysitter in this deal—but he was grabbing the opportunity with both hands anyway.

Besides, he liked Ryan a great deal, and he enjoyed racing. His brothers had a number of clients who were involved in the sport, and he was a fan when he could break away from work to watch it on TV. But he'd never been to a live event.

Friday morning, as he walked up the sidewalk toward the lakeside mansion—there was simply no other word for the stone and brick house rising in an elegant tower before him—his memories tossed him back to when he'd been ten years old.

He'd been pathetic and weak.

Unlike Ryan, he hadn't been skilled at soccer—or anything else.

He'd been diagnosed with asthma. He was sick with allergies, weakened by the medicine to treat his condition. Watching from the window of his family home or the stands of the local stadium, he'd been jealous of his older brothers, who'd excelled at baseball and football. He'd never dreamed of strength or confidence.

And yet he'd found it.

In middle school, when he was just a little older than Ryan and his teammates, he'd met a soccer coach who believed in him, and with his father's help, they'd helped him strengthen his body. Neither his coach nor his father had seen a skinny, weakling. They'd seen a warrior.

Sean liked to think he'd fulfilled that reality, and he hoped he was passing on the skills and confidence he'd acquired to a new generation of boys.

Rolling his shoulders back and pretending he wasn't intimidated, he rang the doorbell of the elaborate house.

A woman he recognized as Ryan's grandmother opened the door. "Hi, Coach." Her eyes twinkled. "Come on in," she said as she stepped back.

"Thanks, Mrs. Richardson." He tried not to gawk as he took in the two-story foyer, a wide, sweeping staircase to the second story and the iron and crystal chandelier that rained light onto the polished wooden floor.

She planted her hands on her trim hips. "I know I've told you to call me Honey."

"Yes, ma'am, you have." But while Mrs. "Call me Honey" Richardson wasn't the vision of any grandmother of his, or anyone else he knew, the intimacy of the nickname was hard for him to say. "But I doubt my mother would be happy if I did."

She patted his cheek. "Any young man who listens to his mother gets an A from me." She started down the hallway, casting him a sassy glance over her shoulder. "You might remind my daughter of that when you get a chance."

Sean grinned. "Love to."

She led him to the kitchen, which seemed warm and homey, despite its size and detailed, obviously custom-made cabinets and high-end appliances. The decor was gold and brick-red, and contrasted nicely with the wall of windows in the back and its spectacular view of the glimmering blue lake beyond.

"Have a seat," she said, extending her hand toward the kitchen table. "Kylie should be down in a minute."

"Thanks."

She slid into a chair across from him. Kylie had gotten her bright blue eyes from her mother, he realized, looking at her. In her elegant crème pantsuit, fair skin and smoothly brushed dark blond hair, she looked like a screen siren from the Forties whose name he couldn't recall. If this is what a man could look forward to in Kylie, Sean figured he'd gladly hang out with her for the next fifty years or so.

But just now, those lovely baby blues were narrowed as she studied him, wincing a moment, then forcing a smile. He'd interrogated criminals and witnesses alike often enough to recognize when some serious questioning was in the works.

"Kylie tells me you and your brothers own a security firm."

"We do."

If she was surprised by his unelaborated answer, she didn't appear so. "Successful?"

"Mostly, though besides me, we have two families— my older brothers'—to support, so we work hard to make it so."

She frowned. "Your brothers are married?"

"They are. Five kids between them, including Patrick, who's on the team with Ryan."

"Is this a date with my daughter or an outing with my grandson?"

The abrupt change in subject made him flinch. The woman would have made a hell of a cop. "Ryan invited me," he hedged. He wanted today to be both, but he wasn't sure where he stood in the face of those penetrating blue eyes.

As a trained observer and investigator it was aggravating and a big ego killer to admit he couldn't read her.

"But you're attracted to Kylie," she said, folding her hands together on the table.

Hands usually said a lot about a person's mood, but hers were still, calm, revealing nothing. "I...Yes." There seemed to be little point in pretending otherwise.

She sighed, looking regretful. "I don't think—"

"Ready to go?" Kylie asked, appearing in the kitchen.

Sean rose, thrilled with her timing. He was pretty sure her mother had been about to warn him off.

His heart kicked him once, hard, as he stared at Kylie. She was dressed simply, in a pair of black pants and a white shirt, but that face didn't need any enhancement. She'd probably be stunning wearing a brown grocery bag. Or a towel.

Or nothing at all.

"See you later, Mom," Kylie said, kissing her

mother's cheek. "Don't stay out too late with Captain Marriman."

Her mother grinned impishly. "Tonight it's Captain Peterson."

When she waved them off, Kylie snagged her car keys off a hook on the wall, then headed through the side door and into the garage. "My mother is very popular at the local yacht club."

"I bet she is."

She stopped, turning toward him, her eyes wide with surprise. "You have a thing for my mother?"

"She's a lovely woman, but I'm into brunettes these days."

"Yeah." Her gaze raked him. "I'll bet you have them lined up around the block."

He stepped closer, until he could smell her perfume, until he could touch her, though he didn't. "I'm only interested in one."

A flare of interest heated her eyes before she looked away. "We need to get going."

When she opened the driver's side door, he moved in behind her. "I'm driving."

"But I need my truck."

"Right. For emergencies." He extended his hand for the keys. "I can drive it."

She angled her head. "Is this a guy control thing?"

"Yes. How'd you guess?"

"I spend every weekend surrounded by forty-three male hotshot control freaks. I ought to recognize the signs by now."

With only a token sigh, she surrendered her keys,

then rounded the SUV and climbed into the passenger seat. Sean knew where Ryan's daycamp was, since the team practiced on the local YMCA's field just down the road, so he started in that direction.

He also knew he had only a few minutes for adult conversation before Ryan and racing became the focus.

"What's it like when the races are in Charlotte?" he asked.

"It's hectic, but it's also great to have all the fans in town. They visit all the racing shops, spend money at the track, malls and restaurants, boost the local economy."

"Clog up the traffic."

"Sure, but I get to sleep in my own bed for two straight weeks."

"Do you usually sleep in somebody else's?"

She whipped her head toward him, shock evident on her face before she noticed his smile. She swatted his shoulder lightly. "I usually spend weekends in a hotel. Or, when my mother can drive to the track, in our motor home."

"Your mom comes to the races? She seems like she'd be more comfortable at a country club than a race track."

"She's pretty comfortable anywhere. She comes mostly to the east coast ones. We drive up in the motor home, and Ryan gets to camp out for the weekend. He loves it and spends a lot of time with the drivers' and owners' kids, hanging out and playing soccer or football in the infield."

"And you get to spend the weekend with your son."

"When I'm not working. My mom is great, watching him when I can't, keeping us all fed and entertained."

"Does she?"

She rolled her eyes, but in a loving, rather than annoyed way. "You should see it. She has her own fan club. Mostly team members and owners. She bakes—pies, cakes, sweet rolls and cookies—every Saturday."

"I'm sure those guys appreciate homemade treats."

"They do beat fast-food apple pies in cardboard boxes. Though sometimes she has ulterior motives— scoping out dates for me."

"Does it work?"

"No," she said coolly.

Dating was obviously a sore subject for her. Which was too bad, because that's exactly what he wanted to talk about. "Maybe you just haven't met the right guy."

She stared out the window. "I don't think that's the problem."

Not knowing how to deal with her sadness, he cleared his throat. "You go on snack runs for Will Branch often?"

That brought her head back toward him quick enough. "No, of course not."

"But you take care of everything for him. Is that really your job description?"

"Are you making fun of me?"

"No way." He shrugged. "I just don't get the PR rep thing. Grown men need somebody to follow them around everywhere they go, making sure they say the right things, handle all the details of their lives, direct them to every destination?"

"Yes."

"Weird."

"The driver's job is to race. My job is to make their sponsor happy, so they will foot the bills for them to do their job. Which is to race. The caretaking is a side benefit." She paused. "For them, not me."

"I don't think I'd like somebody following me around all day." He was the follower, not the followee. Grinning, he looked over at her. "Then again, if *you* were the one following me, I might not mind so much."

"That's a fairly inappropriate thing to say to the mother of one of your players."

Her lips were twitching, as if she might be holding back a laugh, but her eyes were narrowed—like her mother's had earlier.

"If you'd go out with me, you wouldn't just be the mother of one of my players."

Her lips stopped twitching. She pressed them together briefly. "I thought we settled this the other day."

"No, I temporarily set aside the topic to protect the boys."

"Protect the boys?"

"From seeing me beg to date you. I have a kick-butt reputation to maintain, you know."

She blinked slowly. "You're going to beg me to date you."

"If it's absolutely necessary."

"That won't be necessary."

"Really? I know weekends are out, but how about Tues—"

"That won't be necessary, because I'm not dating you."

"Why not?"

"You're my son's soccer coach."

"And dating you would violate my morality clause with the YMCA?"

"Don't be cute." She sighed. "Improbable, maybe even impossible for you, but try."

"I'll settle for irresistible."

She didn't return his smile. She crossed her arms over her chest. "I'm nearly a decade older than you."

"So?"

"Don't you want to date somebody your own age?"

"I want to date somebody I like. I like *you*."

"I like—" She stopped, biting her lip.

His heart rate sped up. "You like me, too."

"You're cute. Didn't I say you were cute? But I—" Grief settled over her face. She looked out the window. "I'm not ready to date."

The age thing didn't worry him in the least. This obstacle, however, was much more dicey.

Though he'd resisted investigating Kylie, he'd done some digging into the life of her former husband, justifying his actions by saying the information was important in dealing with Ryan.

Matt Palmer had been an exceptional cop. Decorated and dedicated. Smart and tough when he needed to be. His death had been a blow not just to his family, but an entire squad and community.

"It's been four years," he said quietly. "You haven't dated at all?"

"A few times," she said to the window. "It hasn't gone well."

Sean pulled to a stop in the carpool line in front of Ryan's daycamp. They barely knew each other. This conversation, touching on her sorrow and pain, was too personal, too much too soon.

His brother was right. Widows with kids weren't his style. Kylie was on a difficult emotional journey. Was he strong enough to help her down that road?

You're not weak. Not anymore.

"Our date would be different," he said, quietly.

"You think?"

"Yes." He reached across the console and grasped her hand. "I'm not asking for a lifelong commitment or undying love, you know. It's just dinner."

"Yeah. Sure." She rolled her shoulders. "Major overreaction, huh?" Trying to smile, she squeezed his hand, then let it go. "I'll think about dinner, okay?"

"Okay."

They waited only a few minutes before Ryan came out, accompanied by one of his counselors. Ryan opened the back door. "Coach Treadway!" he exclaimed, tossing his backpack on the floor of the truck and clambering inside. "It's so cool you're coming with me. You're gonna love the track, and we can go to the garage and watch the guys work on the cars, but you can't touch anything, because—"

"Hey, champ," Kylie said, turning to look at her son. "Remember me? Mom?"

"Yeah. Hey, you let Coach drive your SUV. You never let *anybody* drive it. Well, except that time Will took it, and we did burnouts in the parking lot. Do you know how to do burnouts, Coach?"

"Ah, no," Sean said as they pulled away from the curb.

"Even if he did know how," Kylie said sternly, "you're not getting in a car that does burnouts ever again, remember?"

In the rearview mirror, Sean caught Ryan's eye roll. "Will is a *professional*, Mom."

"He's a professional in a steel-framed roll cage, a custom-made seat, five-point safety harness, head and neck restraints and wearing a helmet."

"Does that mean I can do burnouts in a race car? Cool!"

Kylie whipped around in her seat. "No, it does not. Ryan Mitchell Palmer, you—"

"Chill, Mom. I was kidding. I know I can't get in a race car." He paused until Kylie faced forward again. "At least until I'm eighteen."

"And we'll all do the happy dance when that day comes," Kylie said dryly, rubbing her temples as if she had a headache.

Here was a custom-made opportunity to prove to Kylie that he was different from other guys. That he could be interested in her and still pay attention to her son. "Actually, Ryan," Sean said, "there are racing series for younger kids. There's—"

"Coach Treadway," Kylie said sharply, "I had no idea you were an authority on racing."

"I'm not. But I've heard about it. Mostly they race on dirt, and they make safety a big priority, so—"

"Arthur Sean Treadway." Kylie shot him a furious glare. "There will be no more discussion of my son driving a race car. Of *any* kind. Understood?"

Ryan slunk down in his seat. "You screwed that up, dude," he muttered. "When she uses all three names, you've really messed up."

"Understood?" Kylie repeated.

Sean nodded, saying nothing.

Clearly, he had a lot to learn about widows and kids.

CHAPTER FIVE

With Sean and Ryan at her side, Kylie knocked on the door of the office/locker room/meeting room/lounge in the back of Will Branch's team hauler.

"Come in!" Will called.

Ryan shoved open the door and ran inside before Kylie could move. "Hey, Will, could you help me with the racing game? Honey keeps—" He stopped, his face flushing. "Honey's doing real good. I need help."

Will, who was sitting on the long sofa across the room and slipping on his racing shoes, smiled at Ryan. "She's not beating you, is she?"

Ryan stared at the floor. "Well, maybe…once or twice."

Will stood. Big for a race car driver, he looked so tall and broad next to her small son. Blond, blue-eyed, attractive and single, he and his twin brother, Bart, were especially popular with female fans. As mischievous, sometimes even devious, as he could be, Will was generous with his fans, kind to kids, dogs and grannies. Plus, he loved fast cars, fast food and video games.

Was it any surprise that Ryan worshipped him?

"She's probably practicing while you're at camp," Will said to Ryan.

"You think?"

Kylie walked toward them, pleased Will was interested enough in her son to keep track of his summer schedule. "I wouldn't put it past her."

"Hey, Kylie," Will said, leaning over, brushing his lips across her cheek.

"Will, this is Ryan's soccer coach, S—"

"Arthur Treadway," Sean said before she could finish the introduction.

Will shook his hand. "Nice to meet you, Arthur."

"You, too."

"Yeah, yeah," Ryan said impatiently, tugging on Will's uniform sleeve. "The game. I need—"

"Ryan," Kylie said in a warning tone.

"Please," Ryan said, his blue eyes turning grudgingly polite. "Can you please help me with the game?"

"Sure, buddy." Will ruffled Ryan's hair. "After qualifying." He grinned at Kylie. "Long as Mom approves."

He can *be taught.*

Kylie nodded. "Mom is fine with video games for an hour." She saw the protest rise on her son's face. "Will has other commitments." Probably involving a curvaceous blonde. "An hour's fair."

Ryan tried to look aggravated, but she could tell he'd gotten more than he expected. "Yeah, okay."

Kylie glanced at her watch. "We should head toward pit road. You're tenth in the qualifying order."

"Yeah," Will said. "Let's go. Are you a big race fan, Arthur?" he added as they headed out of the office and made their way down the hauler's narrow hallway.

"I watch it on TV when I can," Sean/Arthur said.

Frankly, the name thing was freaking Kylie out, but she kept moving and clutched her clipboard, containing the weekend's schedule, against her chest.

"You've never been to a race?" Will asked.

"Nope," Sean said. "A friend and I were planning to go the Richmond race a few months ago, but work called me away, so I missed it."

"What kind of business are you in?"

"Security."

"Yeah? Cool."

As they reached the back of the hauler, Kylie turned toward the guys. She put on her most serious, professional face. "The press and fans are outside that door."

"No kidding?" Will said, his eyes twinkling.

"I'm just reminding everybody," she said.

"She means me," Sean said.

Ryan looked up at the two men. "I thought she meant me."

Kylie clenched her fist by her side. She was taking her driver, her son and her son's soccer coach/guy who wanted to date her into the waiting arms of the motorsports press.

As if reporters care about your private life.

She shook aside her paranoia. No one was going

to question why she was hanging around a younger man. No one was going to point their finger at the lonely widow and pity her. No one cared if she was chasing her son's soccer coach like a love-starved fool.

I'm not chasing anybody.

"Kylie?" Will waved his hand in front of her face. "Are we going, or are you plotting a PR stunt I need to know about?"

Kylie raised her chin. "I don't do stunts."

She spun and peeked through the window in the door, noting team members pushing cars, a few fans milling around with cameras, autograph books and pens, plus a couple of well-known print reporters holding minirecorders. She hoped they only wanted to talk about the upcoming weekend. If Will had to answer one more query about where he thought his father had run off to, she feared he'd slug somebody.

She opened the door. "Coach, you and Ryan go first."

"You're a gem, Kylie," Will said quietly in her ear as the other guys walked down the steps. "I like hanging with Ryan and playing games, but there's a hot redhead coming my way later."

Glancing back, she raised her eyebrows. "And I guessed a blonde. Obviously, I need to tune my radar."

"But if you run into any sizzling blondes…"

"Feel free to pass along your unlisted cell phone number?"

"Oh, yeah." Grinning, Will extended his arm toward the door. "Into the fray we go."

"The *fray*?"

"We got a guy named Arthur leading the security detail, so it fits. Is that why you brought him today? You think I need a security guard?"

"To hold back all the redheads and blondes, it couldn't hurt."

"But I don't want to hold them back."

She shook her head ruefully. "Good point. And, no, I didn't bring him for you. Ryan invited him."

"But there are sparks between you two."

"There are *not*."

Will shrugged. "I'd never argue with the woman in charge of my positive public image."

Her gaze flicked to his. "But?"

"The sparks light the room."

He walked though the door before she could argue, and she buried her embarrassment as a group of fans descended on Will and the reporters moved toward her.

She let Will do his charming, budding superstar thing with his fans while she chatted with the reporters. Before they started toward pit road, she pulled Will into the media conversation. Pithy quotes in progress, she glanced over at Sean and Ryan.

Her son was pointing out the garage across the alley from the haulers. He was gesturing; Sean's head was cocked as he listened. Team members rushed by with equipment and cars. Fans gawked. Owners and NASCAR officials had conversations in small, usually separate, huddles.

"…ready to qualify," she heard Will say.

Startled from her personal thoughts, she asked the

reporters to wind up the interview, then hustled Will along to pit road, Ryan and Sean trailing behind.

After passing off her driver to his team, she stepped back with her son. And Sean. Or was it Arthur?

She wasn't sure she knew, or if it even mattered.

"Ryan, little man!" One of Will's team members passed by, giving her son a high five. "You ready to kick Pele's butt yet?"

Though Ryan grinned from ear to ear, he shook his head. "Pele hasn't played soccer in forty years, sir."

"But Ryan's a legend in the making," Sean said, laying his hand on Ryan's shoulder.

Kylie kept part of her attention on Will, now standing by his race car and being interviewed by the TV crew, and part on Ryan and Sean, talking soccer with Will's team. Certainly not a sport to rival racing, football, baseball or basketball in popularity, but lots of guys in the garage had kids who played in local rec leagues, a couple of them on Ryan's team.

Many weekends they played pickup games in the infield or saw each other at local matches. Ryan was one of the lucky ones, though, since his grandmother could bring him to a lot of races, and they could all be together as a family. Despite the high-paying professions, high-profile exposure of the sport and the love and enthusiasm of racing, there were plenty of sacrifices on the home front.

Even Will, who smiled in front of the camera, and who, along with his twin brother, was perched on the edge of a promising career, had baggage. His family was in shambles, and all of the dirty laundry was out for public consumption, amusement and speculation.

His mother, Maeve, was desperately trying to hold on to her social status and dignity, but she had little to smile about these days.

When the TV crew moved on, and Will's team surrounded him, preparing to tuck him into his car for qualifying, Kylie stepped back, sitting on pit wall. After he made his run, provided he didn't wind up on the pole, she could escort him back to his motor home, then relax.

Engine revving, another car roared off pit road, heading out for its qualifying run. It was hot as blazes under the late August sun, and with the infield surrounded by motors, people and asphalt, the temperature was even higher. Hope and anticipation lay thickly in the air for the teams. American flags flew proudly, flapping in the strong, hot breeze.

When one of the driver's sons joined Ryan and they started talking about predictions and strategies, Sean stepped back and moved closer to her. "If you ever get tired of your job, he could do it."

Watching her son's animated face, she nodded. "I know."

Sean looked over at her. "You're raising a great kid."

Unexpectedly, she found herself fighting back tears. Ryan looked so much like Matt, yet he had her gift for conversation and negotiation. "Thanks."

Now was not the time to get weepy. Not only was she working, but she'd promised Felicia she'd make an effort to move on. She'd promised herself she'd stop living in the past.

Knowing noise was always an issue at the track, and not wanting to shout, she was waiting for the qualifying car to roar down the backstretch before she leaned toward Sean. "You introduce yourself as Arthur?"

"I told you, only my close friends and family call me Sean."

"I'm not a close friend or family."

He smiled—slowly, invitingly, and her stomach tightened, then performed a sweet roll. "Then I definitely need to add hot brunettes that I want to date to my list."

She wanted to ignore the attraction, the undeniable chemistry that dominated her thoughts and reactions whenever he was around. But she couldn't quite make herself be that dishonest.

At least not to herself.

She cast a nervous glance toward Ryan. "I'm not hot. And I'm definitely not hot here, when I'm working and my son is two feet away."

Sean shook his head. "No use fighting the obvious."

The mischievous grin, the light in his eyes, the fitted T-shirt over his leanly muscled body and low-slung jeans added devastating images to her weakened state.

"Fourth, Mom!" Ryan shouted, bouncing in front of her. "Will qualified fourth!"

She hadn't even been aware he'd been on the track.

Arthur "Sean" Treadway, as good as he was for her ego, wasn't good for job performance.

"I think there are quite a few cars left to go out," Sean said.

"We'll stay around for a while," Kylie added, casting Sean a grateful glance. Comments like his sometimes brought about arguments between her and her son. "Then I have to get Will his next appointment."

"That's with me," Ryan said, crossing his arms over his chest. "He promised he'd help me with my game."

Kylie barely suppressed a wince. "Right." She hoped Will to remembered his promise.

By the time they'd hustled back to the hauler, Will, thankfully, was more than ready to escape into a video game session with Ryan. Promising to return in an hour, Kylie led Sean outside.

"So, what do you want to see?" she asked him as they headed down the road between the garages and the haulers.

He patted his stomach. "I could eat."

She had several hospitality tent tickets secured to her clipboard for just this sort of emergency. "I can feed you. We'll get something for Ryan, too, then we need to get out of here. I have an early meeting tomorrow."

"He seemed set on watching all of qualifying."

"But I can divert his interest to food. Men are driven by food."

"Are we?"

She raised her eyebrows. "Aren't you?"

He laughed. "Sure. That and…" His gaze slid suggestively down her body. "Other basic needs."

"I'm prepared to deal with hunger."

His hand slid along her waist. "What kind?"

Briefly, she closed her eyes. "The kind that can be filled by hamburgers and/or barbecue."

"A burger will satisfy me—for now anyway."

She hoped she could say the same. Temptation wasn't a familiar feeling for her. At least not until Sean had walked into her life. Now she was a mass of confusing, enticing thoughts.

As they rounded the end of the garage stalls, she waved to a couple of people who called her name, then was stopped twice by other reps. She introduced Sean—as Arthur, which still seemed weird, but it was his preference, after all—then he stood silently by while she talked shop with her peers.

He didn't seem impatient or bored, and he didn't try to monopolize the conversation. One of the guys she'd gone out with several months ago absolutely loved the sound of his own voice, and he'd driven her crazy in twenty minutes. It was probably wrong of her to seek flaws in Sean as well, but the wariness was there anyway. Might as well be honest with herself about it.

She wanted to remember her husband as perfect. Then no one else would ever measure up, and she wouldn't have to risk her heart again.

Of course, self-realization didn't make the emotional obstacles any easier to overcome.

By the time they'd reached the hospitality tent,

gotten their food and were seated at a table in the back corner of the tent, Sean had to be starving. "I'm sorry this took so long," she said, watching him work his way through a double cheeseburger.

"No problem. You're working." He dragged a fry through a puddle of ketchup. "I work alone. It would annoy the hell out of me to have somebody tagging along."

"I'll remember never to bother you on the job."

"I wouldn't take you with me. It's too—" When he stopped, he dropped his gaze briefly. "I couldn't give you my full attention."

Oddly enough, she thought he'd been about to say something else, but what, she had no idea. Silly. She was reading too much into everything today.

"Did one of those lousy dates involve Will Branch?" he asked.

"What?" Shocked by the abrupt change of subject, she stared at him. "What dates?"

"You told me the other day that you'd been on a few dates, and they were lousy. Was Branch one of those guys?"

"No, he's too…"

"Too…"

"Wild." And young. Though Will was thirty, which made him much closer to her age than Sean was. She frowned. Why did they seem reversed maturitywise? "Plus, he's my client. I don't date clients. Why do you want to know?"

Sean smiled. "Just wondering if I have to fight him for you."

She fought a smile of her own.

"I could take him. I'm fast, plus I've got my karate training."

"Please don't tell Ryan about the karate. He's been bugging me for months to take lessons."

"He should." He held up his hand when she narrowed her eyes. "Not that I'm telling you how to be a parent, but it's good for discipline and strength building. It's not all high-flying back kicks and board breaking."

She shook her head. "It's too aggressive and dangerous."

"It's the opposite," he argued. "Weren't you concerned about his strength for goal kicks?"

"I don't think this is the way."

"How about I take you—just you, without Ryan—to the dojo where I train? You can meet Master Ling, observe a class and decide for yourself. Any Tuesday, three-thirty."

She couldn't imagine Ryan kicking and punching, even for strength building. Wasn't karate just an elegant form of boxing? But she also admitted she didn't know much about the sport. "Okay, I could go to a class. But don't say anything to Ryan." Then another thought occurred to her. "This isn't a sneaky way of getting me to go on a date with you, is it?"

"No way. This would be me taking Kylie the Mom to karate class." He leaned close to her, his voice deepening. "Kylie the Woman I want to take to a quiet, elegant Italian restaurant and share wine, pasta and longing looks with across the candlelit dinner table."

Oh. Oh my.

Temptation was too mild a definition for him. He was fascinating, alluring, intriguing.

And she was running out of excuses.

As Sean pulled Kylie's SUV into her garage, he glanced in the rearview mirror, noting Ryan was still zonked. The kid had inhaled his double cheeseburger and fries—and wasn't it great they had the same culinary palate?—then promptly passed out in the backseat on the way home from the track.

As great as Ryan was, and important to him regardless of Sean's attraction to the boy's mother, he couldn't wait to tuck the kid into bed, so he could finally have a private moment with Kylie. Being the trained observer he was, he also noted the black Mercedes sedan that had been parked in the garage earlier was gone. Mrs. Richardson, also known as the vibrant and curious Honey, was still on her date.

Now, if he could work some magic on the beautiful, if wary, brunette sitting beside him…

She cast a glance at her son. "I hate to wake him."

"Maybe we don't have to," Sean said. "I can carry him to his room."

Her gaze slid to his and held for a long moment. "Okay."

Sean turned off the truck's interior lights, so they wouldn't come on when he opened the door.

As he lifted Ryan into his arms, he abruptly realized what Kylie's intense stare had been about. While he'd tucked his nephews into their beds many times, usually tossing them on the mattress to their delighted squeals of glee, a sleeping child was precious and vulnerable. Trusting someone to that intimate duty implied a sense of faith that he'd yet to earn with the Palmer family.

Swallowing his nerves, he followed Kylie through the kitchen and up the back stairwell. They walked silently across the dimly lit breezeway over the living room, then down the hallway to the third bedroom on the left. Only a night-light in the corner shone, so Sean could only make out navy blue walls, shadowed posters, a desk, dresser and double bed with a soccer net as a headboard.

After Kylie turned down the sheets, he gently laid Ryan on the bed. His hair was tousled, his eyes closed, his face relaxed. Sean was used to watching his team of boys in full throttle, so the picture seemed odd, but comforting.

What was it like to watch your child sleep? To know you were responsible for his care, security and comfort? To know he relied on you for guidance and wisdom? To know that some day you'd have to let him have his independence? To know you were training him, constantly, to leave you and function on his own?

Scary, he decided, watching Ryan's chest rise and fall beneath his rumpled red T-shirt. Scary and amazing.

His eyelids fluttered. "Coach?" he asked, obviously confused.

Sean's breath caught, and, for a moment, he

wasn't sure how to respond to those dazed eyes. Some instinct urged him to move. He laid his hand on Ryan's shoulder. "You're home, buddy. Your mom's right here."

On impulse, not knowing exactly why, he leaned down, kissing his forehead before backing away and letting his mother say good-night.

Another instinct told him Kylie might want a few minutes alone with her son, so he retraced his steps and went downstairs. Only one lamp was on in the living room, so if he stood close to the windows, he could see the blackened lake behind the house.

There was a dock jutting out into the water and a boat bobbing in the water beside it. The boat was good-sized. About twenty-four feet. Did Kylie know how to pilot it?

He'd bet his black belt she did.

She was very self-sufficient.

Yet she worried about exposing Ryan to a sport she thought of as dangerous. Karate certainly wasn't. The principles were rooted in defense, peace and self-awareness.

But there were certainly dangers to him, to his job. He'd almost slipped earlier by telling her he'd never take her to work with him because it was too risky. Not as much as police work, since they were often called to respond to emergencies they had no control over. His job—hunting criminals, subsidizing a vigilante form of justice—had much more freedom. He could choose his strategy, pick his moment. Most often, he set up his operation silently and carefully, surprising his target, taking him or her into custody with relative peace and hardly any struggle worthy of TV drama or a reality show.

And that was crap.

There was always an element of unpredictability. The kind that left a good agent—or cop—vulnerable to danger. To death.

Because he was used to the dark, used to listening to sounds other people dismissed, he knew the moment she stepped out of Ryan's room. He heard her footsteps as she moved down the hall and stairs. As she grew closer, he scented her, the sweetness of flowers with a hint of musk. Innocent and sensual at the same time.

He didn't turn, knowing she'd speak more openly to his back.

"No man," she said quietly, "no man not related to him, has ever done that before."

He watched the shadowed water ripple on the lake and fought for a casual tone. "I figured."

"It was nice." He sensed her moving toward him. "I didn't expect it to be, but it was."

Turning, he found her close, within touching distance. He didn't want to move too quickly, but he wasn't about to ignore a golden opportunity. "He's a great kid. Any man would be proud to tuck him in at night." He cupped her cheek in his hand. "You just have to give him a chance."

"I'm—" She pressed her lips together. Then, lifting her face to his, she said, "I'm trying."

"Try harder," he suggested, covering her mouth with his.

As he pulled her toward him, she laid her hand on his chest. He breathed in her sweet scent, the lushness of her figure pressed against his body. The closeness he'd craved was here, the need and desire all apparent in their touches and sighs.

But he still wanted more.

He wanted to know how she felt, the emotions that lingered behind those deep blue eyes. He wanted to know why she was kissing him. Was she full of desire, or simply sad and lonely? What spell had she cast over him that he didn't care either way as long as he could hold her?

Suddenly, she jerked back, her breath heaving, her eyes wide, bordering on terrified. "I can't do this. Ryan is upstairs."

In that moment, he realized she hadn't been intimate with any other man since her husband's death. A simple kiss shouldn't have her in a panic.

Four long years of heartache and being alone.

Baggage. Lots of baggage with Kylie.

But, even as she pulled away, he didn't want to. He had no desire to leave her, to find another woman with less complications and problems to work through. There were plenty of women he could enjoy, but he couldn't care less about seeking them out. Even though they wouldn't mind what he did for a living, or that his job of the moment was finding Hilton Branch. Hell, other women would probably be intrigued, maybe even fascinated.

Didn't matter. He wanted Kylie. And he wanted

to find out why he wanted her almost as much as he wanted to touch her again.

"Have dinner with me next week," he said.

"I—" She shook her head and stepped back. "No, I can't."

"Why not?"

"Because I don't date."

"Oh, right. You have a list. Tell me, is this list of people you don't date long?"

Clearly annoyed, her gaze flicked to his. "I don't have a list."

"Sure you do. No clients or soccer coaches. Who else?"

"No cops," she whispered.

"That seems like an obvious one, I guess." He angled his head. "Do you always bring up your deceased husband to men who are attracted to you? I bet you do, and I bet it sends most of them running for cover."

Her jaw dropped. "That's none of your business, and rude besides."

"I intend to make it my business." He stepped close, sliding the tip of his finger slowly down her cheek. "And I don't scare easily."

CHAPTER SIX

"I CAN'T BELIEVE I'm doing this," Kylie said, scowling at her reflection in the full-length mirror.

"Dating shouldn't be painful, sweetie," her mother said, walking into the bedroom. "It's good that you're getting out."

Kylie turned, knowing Honey and her moods too well. "But…"

Honey perched somewhat hesitantly on the end of the bed, though her gaze met Kylie's directly. "You're not going to get attached to this boy, are you?"

"Sean may be younger than me, but he's hardly a boy."

"It's just that going out with a younger man can be a nice ego boost for a night or two, maybe a splashy party or charity event, but long-term you'd always be paranoid about a new wrinkle or an extra gray hair. You'd always wonder about someone younger coming along."

Personally, Kylie thought all that depended on the man and how much he valued smooth skin and perfect hair. But she also couldn't deny her mother was voicing some of the very fears she herself had. "Is that from the personal experience of a professional dater?"

Her lips tipped up in a smug smile. "Naturally."

"Don't worry, Mom. It's just dinner."

Which she still hadn't figured out how Sean had talked her into. Friday night, after coming home from Bristol, she'd been firm in her decision that she wasn't going out with him.

Then on Monday, flowers had arrived, followed by a lush chocolate gift basket at her office on Wednesday morning, then a courier package on Tuesday after her weekend in California, containing his resignation as a soccer coach. She'd called him in a panic, only to have him assure her he hadn't sent his resignation to the YMCA, just to her. But he would, if she wouldn't have dinner with him on Wednesday night.

She'd accused him of extortion; he'd laughed.

Secretly, she'd been wildly flattered he was interested in her enough to go to so much thought and trouble. So, like when Ryan gave her his pitiful face over wanting another piece of chocolate cake, she'd caved. They'd have their date, realize their curiosity and chemistry wasn't enough, then move on.

As long as he didn't kiss her, forcing her to—again—melt into a puddle at his feet, she'd be fine.

She took one last look in the mirror. She felt silly in the expensive designer jeans and fitted, bright turquoise top that Felicia had talked her into, though she did like the trendy wedge-heeled sandals. Maybe the outfit did make her look taller and curvier than usual, but she also knew she had no hope of competing with the early-twenties crowd.

Her waist would never be the size it had been before her pregnancy, and her chest wasn't ever going to be voluptuous without major surgery. Still, she was lucky she'd inherited Honey's good metabolism and a small frame. With some light makeup, lip gloss and low lighting, she didn't look too bad.

"Come on, already. You look beautiful," Honey said, grabbing her hand and tugging her from the room. "Not as good as me, of course, but looks like mine only come along once a generation."

"I *am* the next generation, Mom."

On the stairs, Honey cast a glance back, her lips pursed, her brow wrinkled. "Keep that information to yourself. We could be sisters, you know."

"Stop frowning. You'll ruin those Botox treatments."

Honey ground to a halt at the base of the steps. "That's just plain mean."

"As revenge, you could hold back the name of your dermatologist."

"I will." Honey stomped into the kitchen. "And it would serve you right, too. You'll need him one day."

Kylie fought a laugh and followed her mother into the kitchen. At least now she'd go into this date with a smile on her face.

"Hey, Mom," Ryan said, jumping up from the table, "I got my homework done, so I can come with you and Coach Treadway tonight."

Oh, boy. Why did motherhood come complete with a daily influx of minefields to overcome, dance around or avoid?

"I'm afraid not, champ," Kylie said, walking toward him. "It's a school night."

Ryan's expression turned rebellious. "But my homework's done!"

She'd gone with the most logical, less-likely-to-argue reasoning. Which had obviously done her no good. "It's a grown-up night."

"But Coach *likes* hanging out with me."

"I know he does. But not tonight."

Suspicious, her son's gaze raked over her, his disapproval evident. He moved toward her, sniffing the air. "You're wearing perfume. This is a date, isn't it?" He scowled. "You're *dating* Coach Treadway!"

Kylie fought for calm. "We're having dinner."

Ryan looked disgusted. "You're not going to kiss him or anything, are you?"

The cat was pretty much out of the bag on that one, Kylie thought, fighting a guilty flush.

She wasn't sure whether Ryan was appalled by kissing in general, upset that she was spending time with someone else, or protective of his coach hanging out with someone else, even if that someone else was his own mother. "I—"

The doorbell rang, saving her.

"I'll get it," Honey said, all but leaping from the room.

Ryan followed her, and Kylie trailed him. No

telling what was going to happen at the door, and she wanted to be sure she was in charge of it.

Sean was stepping into the foyer when she got there. He had on a beige polo tucked into black pants, a silver-tipped black belt at his waist. Felicia had assured her *casual* meant jeans. Was she under-dressed or was he overdressed?

He looked lean, sexy and amazing. She looked as good as she was going to. But should she offer to change? He couldn't legitimately change, unless they went by his place, so—

"Are you going to kiss my mom?" Ryan asked abruptly, glaring up at his coach.

"Ah, well…" Sean's gaze jerked to hers, pleading. *Welcome to my world.*

This sort of complication/confrontation was just one of the reasons she didn't get involved with guys. *She* didn't really understand the rules, etiquette and pitfalls of dating. How was she supposed to explain them to her ten-year-old?

It's *one* date, she reminded herself, walking as calmly as she could toward the time bomb of emotions lurking in the foyer. After this date, he'd realize how much trouble a widow and son could be. He'd go back to charming miniskirted, barely-legal-age girls, and she'd go back to being repressed and alone.

It was perfect.

Before she could say anything, Honey gripped Ryan's shoulders. "They're having dinner, sweetie."

"But you won't be bored—" Sean pulled a plastic bag from behind his back and handed it to Ryan "—I thought you might like to play a game other than racing."

Thoughts of mom-kissing and coach-bonding apparently forgotten, Ryan dove into the bag and came out with a video game case. "Cool! It's Soccer Extreme!" He turned toward her, his eyes bright with excitement. "This is what I've been saving my allowance for, Mom. I can keep it, can't I?"

With all the gifts Will Branch offered, she'd trained Ryan to ask her before accepting something. He was a boy without a father, she'd always reasoned, and she'd had to set up parameters—mostly for herself and Honey—to keep from ridiculously spoiling him. With her financial security, toys and games could be an easy, temporary fix to everyone's pain and loss.

But all her reasoning and practicality were no match for the covetous expression on Ryan's face at the moment.

"Of course you can keep it." She shifted her gaze to Sean. "Thank you for thinking of him."

His silvery blue eyes warmed, and she felt the heat all the way to her toes. "My pleasure."

It should be illegal for a man who looked that good to say words like *pleasure*. Trying to appear casual and confident—though she felt neither—she snagged her purse off the table in the foyer, then walked toward Sean. "We should probably get going."

After she kissed Ryan and Honey goodbye, they

climbed into his jeep, and she brushed her hand self-consciously down her jean-clad thigh. "Are you sure I'm not underdressed?"

"No." His gaze warmed as he looked at her. "The place we're going is a casual sports bar."

"What happened to candlelight and Italian food?" she asked, feeling stupid, but since she'd thought about little else for the last five days, she needed to know.

"Oh, well, that's a second, maybe even third date, kind of place. For the first, we have burgers at the lake."

"I never agreed to a second or third date."

"You will."

He backed out of her driveway, while she stared at him in astonishment. That slow smile and easy drawl masked a driven, determined man. She should know. She'd seen the same traits in race car drivers dozens of times.

Stopping at the end of the street, he turned toward her, his gaze locked on her lips. "*Can* I kiss you?"

She took satisfaction in the idea that she could put him off balance—and with his own words. "That's probably a second or third date—"

His hand was cupping her cheek and his lips were on hers before she finished her sentence.

She stiffened for a moment, trying to adjust from her need to take things slow, and his to shoot into hyperdrive. She tried not to be seduced by the need fluttering in her stomach and singing through her veins, but failed miserably. The heat of his touch ignited something beautiful and intimate she'd been denying still existed inside her for a very long time.

Nothing and no one could measure up to the way it had been before. And while Sean's touch was undeniably different, it was as electric as she remembered true desire could be.

How have I so quickly and thoroughly have lost control of this situation? she wondered vaguely on a sigh on longing. She was *always* the one in charge.

Not anymore...

And wasn't that just a little bit of a relief? Even if it was also scary?

"It was pretty amazing the first time," he said, leaning back a bit, his voice not quite steady, his fingers still stroking her cheek. "I wanted to make sure my fantasies hadn't exaggerated."

She swallowed and tried to ignore the wild beat of her heart. "Fantasies?"

"Mmm." His gaze dropped to her lips. "They were extremely detailed, and you were the star of each and every one."

Kylie wasn't sure how she should feel about being the star of *any* man's fantasies, much less a man Sean's age. Flattered, certainly. But shouldn't she also be embarrassed?

Would she be embarrassed if any man said that to her or thought of her that way? Did Sean's age really matter in that regard? He'd been trying to tell her it didn't from the first moment they'd met.

She considered herself attractive, but rarely in a purely, womanly sense. She looked nice and professional for her job. She was competent and detailed. She was a good mother and daughter.

But a woman like the one Sean kissed and fantasized about, she hadn't been in years. Maybe never.

If she was going to date—and clearly this was a date—she was going to have to let some things go. She was going to have to get over her itchy, twitchy modesty, where she examined and questioned every move and thought.

Then say something, goofy!

"Don't most of your dates involve miniskirted, barely-legal-age girls?"

His eyes reflected surprise, then amusement. "Are you asking me if I've ever gone out with a woman who wore a miniskirt?"

"I guess so."

"I'm sure I have. I don't remember specifically how old she was. As for the last woman I went out with, I can't remember her name." He stroked his thumb across her lips. "Did I mention, since I met you, you're the only woman I've been able to think about?"

"I think you did."

"Then does the past really matter?"

She shook her head. He had the ghost of her marriage to deal with. Why did she care about the women he'd dated before? She was taking everything way too seriously. Dating was supposed to be fun. Wasn't she entitled to some fun?

"I've been fantasizing about candlelight and Italian food," she said, then smiled, she hoped, flirtatiously.

"We can go there tonight if you want."

She leaned into him, pressing her lips to his in a whisper-light kiss. "That's okay. We can save that for the second date."

SEAN HAD HOPED to sit on the restaurant's deck outside near the lake, but rain had drenched the area the night before, so the moisture had only jacked up the oppressive-to-start-with humidity.

Kylie already had him sweating. He didn't see any point in melting.

She'd ordered a bacon cheeseburger, not some wimpy, girly salad—though he imagined she could do that with style, as well—confirming his observations about her adaptability. Being a professional observer of many types of people, he was glad to have pegged at least that part of her.

She was a business woman, who could no doubt move with the First Rate Auto Loans crowd and their financial backers as easily as she mixed with NASCAR racing fans and other sports people hanging in the bar where they now sat. She talked to multimillion-dollar racing team owners with the same ease she did mechanics. She shifted from mom to executive and back to mom with dizzyingly competent speed. She adored her son and spent much of her time worrying about what was best for him.

But there was so much more that threw him off. She was obviously interested in him, but hesitant to act on that feeling. She lived in the past emotionally, but was sharply in tune with her present in every other way. She was worried about their age difference when he couldn't care less.

"It was really sweet of you to bring Ryan the video game," she said, dragging him from his thoughts. "He's not sure what to make of this...of us."

Yeah? Join the club. "I'm not completely clueless about ten-year-old boys." He spent several days a week with a pack of them, didn't he? His defensive tone wasn't planned, yet it was there anyway. And it was pretty sure he knew why.

He was constantly trying to impress her and convince her he was a good guy, while she, in turn, gave him wary looks and acted as though she might run in the opposite direction at any moment.

"After those mistakes Friday night at Bristol," he added, making an effort to even his tone, "I decided to consult an expert."

"An expert on what?"

"Being a responsible parent. Which my sisters-in-law are." He watched her eyes light up. Was she impressed? "I realized—well, actually, they flat out told me—my talking to Ryan about a racing series he could run in was completely wrong without consulting you first. I also shouldn't have pushed you about the karate training."

She sipped her iced tea and gave him a considering look. "I'm glad you pushed about the karate. I *did* ask you to help him with his strength, and earlier this week I did some research about the sport. I liked what I found out. So you weren't out of line, and I'm sorry if I made you feel that way."

"But…"

"I'm not comfortable with Ryan racing," she said, glancing down briefly. "A lot of his friends race go-carts, and he's done it recreationally, but our lives are already unsettled and full of traveling."

"And it's dangerous," he added, watching her closely, knowing this was a hot button for her.

"Not more than any other sport." She shrugged. "It's just that racing already dominates our lives. I want him to have something for himself."

"And he loves soccer."

She smiled. "He loves soccer. And maybe karate. Do you think I could come next Tuesday afternoon? Three-thirty, right?"

"Yeah. That'd be great. The kids in that class are a little younger, but you'll get the idea." He leaned back as the waitress took their empty plates away. "You could put on a gi and join us."

"That's those white pajama things, right?"

Sean coughed to cover a gasp. "Ah…no. It's a *uniform*. Every part of which has a purpose. The gi makes a beginner feel more confident, a part of the culture. The color of the belt signifies the level of skill. The strength of the fabric allows for durability as well as the freedom of movement, the—"

She held up her hand. "I get it. It's important." She angled her head. "Big faux pas there."

He liked that the comfort level between them was deepening. They could debate, even disagree, and still smile. The desire and attraction hummed between them, but it was natural, not the usual first-date flutters of uncertainty. He felt as if he could share so much of himself with her.

Well, he could be the part of himself that was interested in her, soccer and karate. The professional aspect…that was a whole other deal.

"So you fly out tomorrow night?" he asked.

"Off to Richmond."

"Do you ever get tired of the road?"

"All the time. But I love my job. It allows me to provide generously for Ryan, and it keeps me focused and…busy."

Not thinking about her loss.

The ghost of her happiness with her husband was already an obstacle he didn't know how to overcome. He definitely didn't want to go down that road on the first date, so he changed the subject to the ever-present road construction all over the Charlotte area.

By the time he'd paid the bill and they were heading across the parking lot, he was confident he'd managed to get her to enjoy herself and maybe think of him as a man, not just her son's coach. He needed to figure out how to take another step forward.

He was a strategizer. No way to escape that. It was a vital part of his job and helpful in his coaching. But more, it was ingrained in his personality, in his soul.

And when he wanted something—he glanced at Kylie—or some*one*, he couldn't imagine anything standing in his way.

In the parking lot, a guy several yards in front of them passed under a lamppost.

He looked familiar.

Bringing a cigarette to his lips, he sucked one last drag, then tossed the still-burning butt on the ground. As he did so, his profile was in full view.

It was Mitch Furlow, one of the bail jumpers he'd been assigned to apprehend.

The guy turned away, and Sean doubted his gut for a moment. It didn't seem possible. And yet…

He quickened his pace, watching the guy head toward an old gray sports car at the back edge of the lot. Furlow drove an old gray sports car. License plate 123BDI. Sean had dubbed this Big Dumb Idiot, since it fit the man, and so he wouldn't forget it.

"Are we in a rush to get somewhere?" Kylie asked, lagging behind.

He grabbed her hand and continued his brisk walk, his gaze again darting to the heavyset, dark-haired man as he passed beneath another light in the parking lot. "It's hot. Let's get the air conditioner going."

Heart pounding, he tucked her into the passenger seat of his jeep, then darted around to his side. He wanted the guy to be Furlow, yet he didn't. What would he tell Kylie? *How* would he tell Kylie?

If he followed his target to whatever random location he was headed—and that couldn't possibly be the luxury neighborhood where Kylie lived—she was bound to notice.

The guy was charged with two armed robberies and assault with a deadly weapon—the bat he apparently kept under his passenger seat. He couldn't ignore the possibility of catching him. The cops had been looking for him for three months; Sean had been brought in by the bail bondsman a month ago. This guy should be behind bars, not wandering around among the unsuspecting public.

And the balloon payment was imminently due for the security business. He hadn't brought in Hilton Branch. Until that happened, every jumper was critical, not just to him but his whole family.

Guilt and determination collided in him as they never had before.

Maybe it wasn't him, he thought, though every instinct inside him screamed that it was. Still, there was nothing wrong with following the guy onto the main road and checking the license plate.

"Are you okay?" Kylie asked, angling her body toward him.

"Sure." He made an effort to smile at her. "Sorry. I was thinking about this project at work that's been giving me some trouble."

For weeks I've staked out every sleazy one of the stripper clubs that Furlow haunts. What are the odds of practically bumping into him outside an upscale lakeside sports bar?

"You want to tell me about it?" Kylie asked. "We've talked a lot about my job, Ryan and his sports, but you've been pretty short on details about your work."

And it should probably stay that way. Though that's looking less likely by the second.

"My work's pretty routine most of the time," he

said, starting the jeep's engine, then backing out of the parking space. "I doubt you'd be interested."

Slowly, trying to seem casual, he pulled out of the parking lot behind the sports car. License plate *123BDI*. His heart jolted in his chest.

Well, damn.

"Like you're interested in PR for auto loans," Kylie said.

As Furlow turned right at the traffic light, Sean followed. "I'm fascinated."

He had the target in sight and spoke mechanically, barely aware of what he was saying. The thrill of the hunt heated his blood, sent tingling awareness through his fingers, a feeling almost as needy and as sharp as the desire for the woman beside him.

He moved into the right lane, away from Furlow and let a couple of cars pass him, while still keeping the guy in sight. Kylie talked about a recent promotion they'd done with NASCAR on safe driving and keeping up insurance.

Guilt, evil and ripe, pounded him even as his heart raced with anticipation.

The sports car made a left, then another quick right.

Oh, hell. He's on to me.

"…so the insurance guys didn't want to—"

"Kylie, I need you to trust me." Sean's hands clenched briefly around the steering wheel. Then he ordered his body to gather its resources, to focus, to remember the end goal.

"Trust you? Trust you with what?"

Sean never took his gaze from the car in front of him. "Remember how I tucked Ryan into bed? How I protected and took care of him?"

"Yeah."

"Trust me to take care of you now."

Without waiting for her answer, he punched the accelerator and charged into the night after his target.

CHAPTER SEVEN

As KYLIE WAS THROWN BACK against her seat, she gripped the door handle and glared at Sean. "What are you doing? Slow down. We shouldn't be—"

She stopped as he darted into the opposite lane, went around a slower car, then jerked the wheel back to the right. She wanted to tell Sean he'd left her heart about a hundred feet back, but she couldn't draw enough air into her lungs to speak.

What had gotten into him?

His expression had taken on an intensity she'd never seen before. His eyes were hard, focused, dangerous.

She gripped the handle tighter as he took another hard left, her body jerking with the turn. "Stop," she gasped, finally scared enough, determined enough to not sit passively by while he turned them into a greasy spot on the pavement. "You have to stop."

"I can't," he muttered, staring through the windshield.

Anger followed quickly on the heels of her fear. "Yes, you—"

"Please, Kylie, be quiet. I have to concentrate, so I don't kill us both."

She blinked. What the hell was going on?

She felt as though she'd stepped outside herself, watching his movements, watching herself on a TV or movie screen. She *couldn't* be illegally darting in and out of traffic like a race car driver determined to charge to the front of the pack at Daytona.

They flew down another side street lined with small homes. Kylie wanted to close her eyes, but she remained frozen, hardly able to believe she was caught in this nightmare. Then, ahead of them, a dark sports car hit its brakes and jerked toward the curb.

Sean did the same. "Stay here," he said, slamming the jeep into Park at the same time a man jumped from the car ahead of them and took off running across the lawn.

Sean flung open the door, reached down toward his feet, lifted one leg of his jeans and pulled a small revolver from an ankle holster.

A clinch piece.

Wasn't it odd how the copspeak came back with such ease?

As Sean bolted from the car, Kylie did close her eyes. The past rolled over her, sending chills down her spine. If she looked in the mirror she knew she'd see her eyes standing out starkly from a pale face. She wasn't sure when, or if, she'd ever drawn another easy breath.

Memories assaulted her. Her husband coming home from a late shift, pulling his semiautomatic from its side holster, then reaching down, just as

Sean had done, and unhooking his ankle holster. After locking both weapons in the gun cabinet, he'd walked toward her for a hug.

She recalled his captain presenting the revolver to her at his funeral and explaining what a brave and amazing man her husband had been.

What was happening? What was Sean doing? *Who* was he?

He moved like a cop, she thought now, the signs she'd missed before clicking into place. At the outrageous, furious thought, she opened her eyes.

And saw Sean handcuffing a dark-haired man, holding him facedown in the grass.

"Oh, hell." She shoved open the door and stepped out. "What the devil are you doing?"

His head lifted. She couldn't see his expression, but his words were clear enough. "Get back in the car. Stay there."

She crossed her arms over her chest and leaned back against the car. "No."

"Get in the car," Sean said, his tone cold and commanding. "This is dan—"

"Dangerous? Foolish?" She glanced at the man Sean was jerking to his feet. "Either a bust or seriously illegal."

"A bust?"

"I was married to a cop, remember?"

"Dude," the cuffed man said, straining his neck to look back at Sean, "if you're havin' a spat with the old lady, I can go someplace else. You know, give you some privacy."

"Shut up," Sean said, dragging him toward the car. "You—" he pointed at Kylie "—inside."

By the light of the streetlamp, she could now see his eyes, which had turned bright green with fury, but there was another emotion lurking there that looked like fear.

This is dangerous.

Though she was still angry and confused, she got back in the jeep, closing the door while Sean stood by the hood with his "prisoner." He made a call on his cell phone, and, barely two minutes later, a police cruiser, with its lights flashing, pulled over beside the sports car and Sean's jeep.

Kylie didn't recognize the lean, dark-haired officer, and she wasn't sure whether she was grateful or more concerned by that realization. She cracked the jeep's window, so she could hear the conversation going on outside.

"You got a problem?" the officer asked Sean.

"Nope." Sean grinned. "Solved one." He nodding at the man in handcuffs. "You've been looking for this guy. Mitch Furlow."

"Yeah?" the cop said, looking the guy up and down. "What on?"

"Two armed robberies and assault with a deadly weapon," Sean said.

The cop smirked. "Not a bad haul for the night."

"Anybody gonna read me my rights?" the cuffed guy—Furlow, apparently—asked indignantly. "I got rights, you know."

The cop grabbed Furlow's arm. "Your rights are

my highest priority, pal." He tugged him toward the cruiser, then glanced back at Sean. "You need to come to the station and fill out the paperwork."

Sean glanced at the car; their gazes met for a moment through the windshield before he looked away. "Yeah. Get started. I'll be right there."

As the police car pulled away, Sean climbed into the jeep. "I guess I need to explain."

Ridiculously, as she stared at him and fought the urge to jab him in the stomach with her fist, her anger turned toward Felicia. Felicia, who'd said Sean was an easygoing, free spirit.

Boy, was she ever on the opposite side of the universe with *that* brilliant observation.

Through her years as a cop's wife, she'd encountered a variety of law enforcement types—beat cops, detectives, captains, undercover guys, judges, lawyers and private eyes. Sean fell into none of those categories.

"I get it. You're a bounty hunter," she said coldly. "No explanation necessary. Now take me home."

SEAN SAID NOTHING for several minutes as he drove through the streets of Mooresville, heading toward Kylie's house. He'd screwed up in a monumental way. He'd always known he'd have to explain about his job. *Eventually.*

But he'd hoped to establish a tighter bond between them first. He'd hoped she would know him better and understand that, though his aspect of his family's security business was unusual, it was fairly safe if you were good and careful. And he was.

He'd never anticipated her witnessing the shadier sides of his profession firsthand.

"What would you have done if Ryan had been in the car with us?" she asked quietly before he could figure out how to begin explaining.

Gripping the steering wheel, he considered his answer carefully. He'd been lying since he'd met her. That ended now. "I don't know."

"Then this conversation is over. I don't want you anywhere near me or my son."

He glanced at her. "That's a pretty hard line, Kylie."

"Yeah, well, I'm a pretty hard woman when it comes to mine and my son's safety."

"I protected you," he said. "You were perfectly safe."

She crossed her arms over her chest. "That wasn't for you to decide and control."

"No, it wasn't. I'm sorry I didn't tell you the complete truth about my job. I should have. I know I should have. But it's not like that all the time. Tonight was…a fluke."

"That fluke caught you in a lie. A big, fat, serious lie." She sent him a furious glare. "I told you I didn't date cops."

"I'm not a cop."

"No, you're a glorified vigilante."

The insult struck hard. He performed a service. A paid service, but still one very few people were willing to undertake to protect their communities.

Though there was no denying their business needed money, he and his brothers believed in the value of what they did. They protected families from those who had no regard for anyone but themselves. "I do more than chase cars and tackle people in yards. I have a P.I. license. I—"

"Congratulations. When you decide to focus on sneaking around after spouses who are sneaking around, call me."

Sean ground his teeth. There were P.I.'s who specialized in that area, of course. No doubt many of them were lucrative, but he had no desire to delve into that bordering-on-sleazy department. Thankfully, he didn't have to in order to pay his bills. His skills lay in another direction.

Though if he didn't find Hilton Branch soon, he might have to lower his standards.

He'd have to confess his connection there, too. That is, if Kylie ever agreed to acknowledge his presence again after tonight.

One battle at a time, man.

"I'm not a vigilante," he said. "I'm a security specialist."

"Bounty hunter."

The fact that plenty of women would think his job was cool and exciting only annoyed him further. He couldn't fall for any of *those* women; oh no, he had to fall for the one who said *bounty hunter* with the same disgust most people reserved for *gutter cleaner*.

Is that what you've done? Fallen for her?

Maybe. He was certainly listing to one side.

"I'm a security specialist," he said firmly. "I don't spend most of my nights chasing bad guys down dark alleys."

"*My work's pretty routine most of the time.* You said that to me earlier. And that's bull. I go to an office every day, I make phone calls, write press releases and send e-mails. I order T-shirts and ball caps with Will's sponsor First Rate Auto Loans logo printed on them. I contemplate the advantages of radio versus TV interviews. *That's* routine."

"My job involves a lot of research and planning. I search public records, go to the library, surf the Internet. I talk on the phone and exchange e-mails. When we get wild and crazy at the office, my brothers make appointments with clients, corporate executives and individuals to discuss the best ways to protect their families and businesses with our security systems." He pulled into her driveway and threw the jeep into Park, angling his body to face her. "Why is what we do so different?"

She reached into her purse and pulled out her PDA, waggling it in front of him. "Compared to that revolver strapped to your ankle, I'd say there's a serious difference."

He sighed. Would the grief in her past always rule her? Was he crazy to think he could overcome her prejudices? "I'm careful. I don't take unnecessary chances."

"Don't act like I'm naive or stupid," she snapped as she jumped out of the jeep, slamming the door behind her and then stomping toward the front door.

He followed her. "You're neither. You're—"

"I was married to a cop," she said, whirling toward him as they reached the porch. "I know about people who love skirting the law, I know there are scumbags and violent crazies lurking out there. I've seen my husband and his friends struggle against the evil, dark side of mankind. I know somebody has to step up and fight that fight, and I know they get very little appreciation for their sacrifice." She drew a deep breath, hitching her purse on her shoulder and turning away. "But I did my time, and Matt gave his life. I figure Justice owes me instead of the other way around."

He wasn't prepared to deal with this kind of pain. He wanted to turn away. He *should* turn away.

But his family didn't abandon him when he needed them most, and he simply couldn't ditch Kylie.

When he was a kid, when he was dealing with his asthma, how had he made himself strong? He'd trained. He'd pushed past his supposed limits. And he'd gotten stronger.

Kylie would get stronger, too. And he would help her do it.

He reached for her hand, but she pulled away.

"Dinner was nice," she said, looking at him and *through* him. "But this isn't going to happen between us. I have to protect my son. I'm sorry."

And protect yourself, Sean thought, bleakly watching her slip into her house.

KYLIE DID what she always did when she was troubled. She worked.

Bags packed for Richmond, she headed into downtown Charlotte and her office. She'd leave for the airport directly from there that afternoon. Since she'd be spending the weekend alone, she wasn't all that anxious to leave. And while normally Kylie didn't mind a weekend by herself, this one had lousy timing. But this race was the final chance to make the Chase and Kylie had to keep Will focused.

At the office, she made it through most of her in-box, dealt with a brief crisis in finding toner for her printer, and had a quick conversation with her colleague Anita Wolcott about some joint interviews for Will and Bart.

She didn't allow herself to think about Sean until she was seated on the plane heading north. She still couldn't believe he'd lied so easily and effectively. She couldn't believe she'd been so trusting, so unobservant and clueless about his job. After being married to a cop for eight years, she knew how they moved and spoke.

Even when she and Matt had gone out to dinner, laughing and enjoying each other, his eyes could narrow in an instant on anything out of the ordinary. He'd always maintained an extra layer of watchfulness that regular people simply didn't possess.

Sean had the same sense.

But she'd obviously been so dazzled by Sean's gorgeous face and distracted by their chemistry, she'd gone momentarily blind and deaf.

Many times during the night she'd considered

transferring Ryan to another team, to make a clean break, but either her pride or her motherly instincts held her back.

Pride told her she shouldn't assign too much importance to her and Sean's disastrous date. Instincts reminded her Ryan worshipped Sean, and her son had obviously been uncomfortable with his mom dating his coach, so it was just as well that things hadn't worked out.

No big deal. One more bad date to file away with the rest. He wasn't the man she'd perceived him to be, the one he tried to make her believe he was. He wasn't laid-back and easygoing, he was dark and dangerous.

She wouldn't think about his warm smile, that hot kiss or even the way he'd been so worried about her during the big takedown the night before.

As she strode through the airport, she checked her messages and discovered yet another one from Felicia. She certainly wanted the scoop on the date, and since Kylie had no idea how to explain everything that had happened, she hadn't returned her call.

In the meantime, though, she'd discovered an eternal truth.

A man who caused a woman to avoid her best friend was a man to be avoided.

By the time she was on the interstate in her rental car and heading to the hotel, guilt and loneliness had gotten the best of her, so she called Felicia.

"I presume you're not bleeding on the side of the road," she said by way of a greeting.

"No, I'm just on the road. In Virginia. It's cooler up here than at home. But not much."

"You don't seriously think I called twelve times to talk about the weather, do you?"

"I guess not."

After a couple of seconds passed, Felicia demanded, "So…out with it."

"I will. Don't rush me. And stop tapping your foot."

"How do you know I'm tapping my foot?"

"I know you."

"Oh, wow, you slept with him, didn't you? How was it? I bet it was—"

"No, I didn't sleep with him." Kylie pulled the phone away from her ear briefly to stare at it, as if it might have an idea where that crazy idea had come from. "Have you lost your mind? This was our first date."

"So? When the chemistry is there, sister, I say go for it."

Felicia was a lot more comfortable "going for it" than Kylie was. Not that she was intimate with every man she met, but she didn't have all of Kylie's baggage and conservative hang-ups, so she had a much more active social life. Kylie hated to burst Felicia's bubble about something developing between her and Sean, but it was better to rip off the bandage.

"We're not going out anymore. He lied to me. About his job. He's a bounty hunter."

Felicia coughed. "You're kidding?"

"I wish I was. We were leaving the restaurant last night, and he sees a bond jumper in the parking lot. We take off after him, and he winds up chasing the guy, throwing him to the ground and handcuffing him."

"*Oh*. Oh, wow."

Hearing the feminine breathlessness in her friend's voice, Kylie clenched her jaw. "It wasn't exciting. It wasn't the late night movie. It actually happened, and it was disturbing and horrifying."

"Horrifying? Oh, come on. It sounds pretty exciting to me."

"What if Ryan had been in the car? The man carries a *gun*, Felicia. He chases dangerous people for a living. He's a dangerous man."

"Matt carried a gun," she said primly. "Was he dangerous?"

"That was different."

"How? He was a cop when you met him, wasn't he?"

"Sure, but—"

"And he, his gun and his dangerous profession were part of Ryan's life for years."

The grief rose unexpectedly, grabbing her by the throat. "And look where that got us."

"You can't live in the past forever, Kylie," Felicia said, her tone growing gentle. "Another guy will come along with dark hair, and you'll say you can't see him because he looks too much like Matt. You need to at least admit you're not afraid of Sean's job as much as you're afraid of how he makes you *feel*. I haven't seen you smile and flush over a guy in four years. Any man who can make that happen is a winner in my book."

Kylie said nothing, staring through the windshield and into the darkened sky. She couldn't close her eyes and fully relive the moments when Sean had leaned toward her, pressing his lips to hers, as she had every day for the last week, but that didn't stop the heat from racing through her body.

"He *lied* to me," she said weakly, offering up the argument her pride had clung to.

"Yeah. Bad move there. Bet he comes up with a great way to apologize."

Kylie groaned. "You're not helping."

"Yes, I am. In fact, when you guys decide to get married, I'll even give you the best friend discount."

"Are you listening to me? There's not going to be a second date, much less a wedding."

"Yeah, yeah. When you get back I want to meet him. Let's do chocolate martinis at the Lakeshore Grill on Tuesday."

"I'll be there, but I'll be alone."

"Whatever you say." Though clearly she didn't think that was true. "I have just one last question— how sexy did he look tackling the bad guy?"

Now Kylie really did close her eyes, though only for a brief moment. "I was in fear for my life. I didn't notice."

"Come on. Details."

"I'm hanging up now."

And she did, still seething. She was a responsible woman and parent of a young child. She would *not* get involved with men who carried guns for a living. No way, no how.

Exciting? Ha! Try ridiculous.

No woman went back for that kind of torture.

And it wasn't as if this was a transitional thing until he worked his way up to something more secure. His family business was security. While his brothers met with clients, he tracked the bad guys down dark alleys, no matter what he said.

He obviously loved his job. Hell, he all but admitted he wouldn't have hesitated to go after his fugitive even if Ryan was in the car. Good for him. Her community was probably a safer place with him around.

But she wasn't having any part of it.

With her self-righteousness firmly in place, she checked into the hotel, bought a sandwich and pasta salad in the lobby deli, then headed to her room.

She slept hard and, thankfully, dreamless, probably because she'd slept so little the night before. By the time she'd parked at the track's infield lot and was striding confidently toward Will's motor home Friday morning, she almost felt normal. Pre-Sean.

There was no need to think about, much less get worked up about, a guy she'd known only a couple of weeks.

As she walked through the drivers' and owners' lot, she reviewed the schedule for the day. There was a short driver's meeting before practice where

NASCAR was addressing the troubling trend of aggressive driving. After the morning practice, they were attending a meet-and-greet sponsor function in the hospitality village.

Since Will's father had skipped town with his bank's money, taking the sponsorship dollars along with him, she and Will were jumping through any available hoop to please his new sponsor. Then there was afternoon practice, followed by qualifying.

In between all that, she'd run interference between Will and the press, and not just the motorsports media, who stuck to questions like, *How do you feel about your team's chemistry?*

No, she also had to wade through gossip columnists, who wanted insider information on Hilton Branch's mistress, Alyssa Ritchie, and her scandalous book. *And* there were crime beat reporters, all of whom were more fascinated by Branch's continued MIA status than Will's qualifying efforts. There had even been a ballsy P.I. who'd posed as a local newspaper reporter to try to question Will about his father's whereabouts.

It was a sick, sick world.

Of course thinking about P.I.'s brought her thoughts back full circle to Sean.

Shaking off the vivid picture her needy libido provided her brain, she knocked on Will's door.

Which Sean opened.

"Hi, gorgeous." He grinned, leaning against the doorjamb. "Missed me, huh?"

CHAPTER EIGHT

"How DID YOU get here?" Kylie demanded, glaring up at him.

For a second, Sean debated whether showing up was a good idea. He hadn't expected Kylie to welcome him with open arms, but the fierce, angry expression on her face took him back a little. "Nice to see you, too, darling. Come in, have a seat."

She stalked past him and surveyed the living room/kitchen. "Where's Will?"

"In the back getting dressed," he said, closing the door. He figured they'd need some privacy for the next few minutes.

"How did you get here?" she repeated, whirling to face him, her voice low, but still fuming.

"Will's team's jet. Nice. Zipped up here last night. No security lines, big, reclining seats and premium liquor." He sat on the sofa, stretching his arms across the back. "I started to call you when we got in, but Will brought along a *guest* for the weekend, so I volunteered to be their designated driver and look out for them." He raised his eyebrows. "I figured you could use the night off."

"I don't need your help to do my job." She planted her hands on her hips. "Which does *not* involve taking my driver out clubbing. Do you have any idea how busy his day is?"

"Don't worry, Mom, we were in by midnight."

"That's not the point. You had no business—" She stopped, pressing her fingers to her temples. "How did you get on Will's team's jet? Somehow, I doubt you thumbed a ride on the runway."

"Did you know you're beautiful when you're sarcastic?"

"Answer the question."

He should have known charm wouldn't get him anywhere with Kylie. "No big secret." He shrugged. "My brother knows Gideon Taney, owner of Taney Motorsports. He called in a favor."

"So you flew in to supervise Will's date?"

"I came to see you."

Her gaze jumped to his. "You shouldn't have. I'm working."

He leaned forward, bracing his elbows on his knees. "I won't bother you. I just wanted a chance to talk to you, to explain."

"That's not necessary. You—"

"Hey, Kylie," Will said, walking toward them. "Don't say I never return favors."

"Hey." She angled her head. "What favor?"

"There's a long list of ones you've done for me. It was time I did one for you." He nodded at Sean. "Don't let me interrupt the happy reunion." His eyes glittered with amusement. "I can get myself to the drivers' meeting."

As he walked out the door, Kylie blasted Sean with a scowl. "What did you tell him?" she whispered.

Sean rose and moved toward her. He had completely miscalculated this whole thing. "That Ryan wasn't coming this weekend, and we were hoping for a little…ah, private time."

"You—" She spun away from him, her jaw rigid with fury. She stomped to the door. "I take it back. An explanation *is* necessary. Twenty minutes, behind the tire building, be there."

She slammed the door.

"Is this a rumble or a conversation?" Sean asked himself, pushing his hand through his hair.

Walking the path of Hilton Branch's last known steps seemed simple by comparison. So, for the next nineteen minutes, he might as well get to his job. Using his connection to Taney to get to the track was twofold.

He knew he needed to talk to Kylie and convince her his job wouldn't stand in the way of their being together. He could feel her longing to step outside her comfort zone, and he'd gotten her dip a toe, testing the dating waters. Then he'd sent her running the other way with the bounty fiasco.

It was vital that he try to draw her out again ASAP—or else risk losing any chance they had completely.

But he'd also come to the track to show her he didn't need her to complete his current assignment. When he got back on her good side—and he fully intended to make that happen—he wanted her to know he wasn't attracted to her because of her NASCAR connections. He hadn't asked her out simply to get to the people who knew Hilton Branch best. He could handle this case on his own.

Still, they'd certainly have to get around to discussing his part in the Branch case, but he was waiting until he was more secure in their relationship.

Until she was actually speaking to him and not confronting him.

With he credentials in place, courtesy of Will, he headed out of the motor home and into the garage area. He'd toyed with the idea several times that Hilton Branch might disguise himself and appear at the track to see Will and Bart race. He had enough arrogance in himself and pride in his sons to try it. Keeping an eye out for a suspect, though, was as easy as breathing, so he concentrated on looking for anybody he knew, anybody he could probe for information about Branch's whereabouts.

"Hey, Arthur!"

He turned and spotted a mechanic from one of the teams. He'd been to the office recently, inquiring about a security system for his home. He was gone so often he'd wanted to make sure his wife and newborn daughter were safe.

Name, name. What was his name? His brothers were so much better at customer relations than he was.

"Hey…Chris," he said as he approached, thanking whatever crew chief or owner had mandated monogrammed names on pockets. "Your system's going in next week, right?"

"On Tuesday," Chris said as he shook Sean's hand. "You guys have been great. With me on the road so much, I'll sleep a lot better."

"How's the baby?"

His dark eyes lit up. "Perfect. Unless she's crying, then I take her out to the garage and show her the sports car I'm restoring. She loves it."

She loved the attention from her daddy. With his huge family, Sean had witnessed plenty of crying babies. A little food, a little song, a little jiggle… the combination usually worked. Maybe he ought to add some chrome and engine-gazing to his routine.

"Where're you on the Hilton Branch pool?" another mechanic asked as he walked up, a notebook in his hand.

Chris winced. "Not sure, Joe. Meet Arthur Treadway. He and his brothers own the security company I was telling you about."

His gaze sharp, Joe shook Sean's hand. "Security?"

"Like alarm systems," Sean said smoothly. He didn't want to pique the interest of the guy who'd started a Branch pool. "Pool for what?"

"Where Branch's gotten himself off to." Joe flipped open his notebook to show Sean a chart with names of locations along the top and dollar amounts down the side. Basically, you could bet on the city/island of your choice, then back up your guess by dollar amount. Fifty bucks and Bermuda seemed to be the popular choice. "You want in?"

"No," Chris said before Sean could respond. "Don't take this outside the team."

Shrugging, Joe tucked his notebook under his arm. "Gotta keep those winnings in the family."

"That's probably smart," Sean said. "What's your theory about Branch's whereabouts, Joe? If you started the pool, you must have a hot tip."

"Oh, yeah." Joe grinned. "Guy like Branch? After all this time, he's sippin' mai tais on some beach in the South Pacific about now. Lot of people feel the same way. The pool's full of islands."

"What kind of guy is Branch?" Sean asked, keeping his tone casual. "You know, what about him makes you think he'd go to the beach?"

"He has that Texas swagger thing goin' on, you know? Always braggin' about the beach houses he owned."

The ones now all foreclosed by the bank. Branch wasn't hiding out in any of those properties.

"I don't know how he's kept himself under wraps this long," Joe continued. "Never was quiet for more than twenty seconds."

Joe's observations were in line with Sean's, which was one of the reasons Sean was always on the lookout for Branch in disguise. Pride was a big motivator with him. Pride and arrogance. He wanted to see those boys of his race. To see them make the Chase for the NASCAR Sprint Cup.

Chris shook his head. "You guys don't know

where Branch is. You're just saying the islands because that's what *you'd* be doing with all that cash."

"True, true," Joe said. "But I'd never have left a hot chick like that woman of his behind. Saw her on one of those mornin' talk shows, promoting her book. She'd look pretty awesome in a bikini."

Sean knew the guys were talking about Alyssa Ritchie, Branch's mistress, not his graceful, dignified wife Maeve. Though he smiled at the guys talking, his gut clenched. The whole business was sordid and embarrassing, and he felt for the supposedly close-knit family whose lives had all crashed because of one, idiotic, selfish man.

When he got his hands on Hilton Branch, his first instinct would be to punch him in the face.

"Sorry about that," Chris said as Joe walked away. "This Branch bank scandal is back in the headlines with the publication of Alyssa Ritchie's book. It's a big topic in the garage. Me, I'd rather make the Chase, but a lot of people would rather…"

"Focus on somebody's else's misery?" Sean finished for him.

Chris looked relieved. "Yeah."

They talked a couple more minutes, but Sean was conscious of the fact that Chris was working and his focus had to be on his team.

And Sean had a rumble behind the tire building to get to.

He wandered around the garage area for a few more minutes, putting on his best awestruck fan expression. He kept an eye out for Hilton, of course, but he also appreciated the experience of the behind-the-scenes look he was getting into a vibrant, wildly popular sport.

The growl of a single engine when the team fired it up to listen for the slightest ping, ding or misfire. The team members pushing their car toward pit road, weaving through fans, officials and other team members. The anticipation hanging thick in the air, with every mechanic, driver and team owner gazing at the start/finish line, wondering, hoping, their car would sail across first.

Reluctantly, he left the bustling area and headed toward the tire building. By the time Kylie strode around the corner, he was leaning against the concrete block wall, in a spare shadowed area to escape the already escalating temperature.

"All safe and sound at the drivers' meeting?" he asked, not looking up but typing a text message on his cell phone.

"I'm not a babysitter," she said, sounding defensive.

"Didn't say you were." He sent the message, then tucked his phone into his pocket. She looked so damn cute standing there with her defensive, yet still somehow hostile expression in her liquid blue eyes. He wanted to pull her into his arms even as he debated the sense of his attraction to her and the complicated emotions she inspired in him.

If he was going to scale the wall she'd built around herself, he was going to have to be very clever. And very lucky.

"Do you want to start this talk, or you want me to?" he asked her calmly.

"We're not talking about anything, buster. I'm going to *tell* you how it is."

Sean twisted his mouth in annoyance. "Don't talk to me like I'm ten, Kylie. I'm a grown man. You can't push me around so easily."

Her cheeks burned red. "Are you implying I push my son around?"

"No, I'm saying straight out you push *everyone* around." He softened his tone. "You push them away."

Her mouth moved, but no sound emerged. He doubted she'd been in that position often.

"Now, do you want to go first, or should I?"

"Don't tell people we're dating," she said through clenched teeth. "Especially people I work with."

"But we are."

"We're *not*. I told you the other night that I don't want to see you anymore. Don't you remember?"

"Oh, I remember, I just misunderstood. I thought you were angry, and I figured you'd forgive me."

"I—"

He loved watching her struggle with those inborn Southern manners. How exactly did you tell someone you weren't willing to forgive them?

"There's nothing to forgive," she said finally.

"Good. Since we're back on track, I'd like to remind you I never got a good-night kiss." He pursed his lips and closed his eyes.

"You're completely insane. We're not back on track. We're not…anything."

He opened his eyes and gave her his best hurt expression, the one he'd been using effectively on his mom since he was Ryan's age. "You're still angry about me taking you on a retrieval."

"*Retrieval.* You make it sound like you hauled out the garbage to the backyard."

"I did. You're angry."

"I was." She sliced her hand through the air. "My being upset by you chasing that guy isn't the problem. It's your job in general. It's too risky for me and Ryan."

"I wouldn't risk Ryan."

"I asked you the other night if you would have chased that guy if Ryan had been in the car. You said you didn't know. That's pretty damn risky."

He sighed. If he was going to be with Kylie, he had to stop thinking like a bounty-hunting bachelor and start thinking like a parent. But even as a parent, he wouldn't want guys like Mitch Furlow running loose. Plus, a parent had to worry about paying the bills, and his bounties helped provide for him and his brothers' families.

"I know you've got a job to do," she continued. "I understand these people need to be behind bars, but I won't sacrifice my son to the cause."

"These guys shouldn't be mixing among the general public. Do you feel safer with them on the street?"

"As a citizen, I want you to catch them. As a mom, though, my son *can't* be involved. Are we clear?"

He would never do anything to hurt Ryan. "Clear. I promise not to involve Ryan in my work in any way."

"No retrievals with him in the car."

"Agreed."

"And you can't tell him what you really do."

"But—"

She shook her head. "I don't want him to know."

"Fine." It wasn't as if he ran around town bragging anyway. Only the cops and the criminals knew what he did, and Ryan wasn't likely to mix with any of them. He brushed back his lingering concerns that she was barely tolerating his job, knowing if she didn't accept what he did, she couldn't really accept him. She would understand in time. "So, for dinner tonight, I thought we'd—"

"Dinner? Who said anything about dinner?"

"I did. Just now."

"We're not going to dinner."

Now he was genuinely confused. "We settled my job issues. Is there some *other* problem between us?"

"We settled your job issues as they relate to *Ryan*, not me."

Okay, so he was going to have to be very, *very* clever.

He looked straight at her. "Come on, Kylie. We're going out. We'll have fun, go to dinner. I wouldn't mind repeating those kisses. I'd like to try to talk my way into your bed. I don't expect more than that. Do you?"

She studied him for a long moment. "No, I guess not."

"So do you really have to worry about the risks of my job?"

"Those risks were pretty up close and personal Wednesday night."

"That was a fluke. It won't happen again." Unless Hilton Branch walked up to them during dinner some night. But he doubted he'd have to chase that guy through the streets. "Or maybe you already care so much that you're worried about losing me?"

"Of course not," she said quickly.

You could have at least thought about your feelings for me for two seconds.

She paced away, then back. "I just don't understand why. Why do you want me?"

"I have no idea. You're stubborn, way too cautious and hard to please." Smiling, he reached out, brushing his finger down her cheek. "But maybe I'm drawn to the devotion you have for your son and your mom. Maybe I like your smile, even if it does take some effort to make it appear. Maybe I think you're graceful, smart, beautiful and sarcastic. Maybe I admire the way you watch out for everybody around you."

"Maybe it's just the challenge," she said. "The thrill of the chase."

"See, stubborn." And it wasn't the chase, though he wished it were that simple. "Could be. Only one way to find out."

Her lips twitched, and he finally relaxed. "You're stubborn, too, you know. You never take no for an answer."

"We're perfect for each other."

"Don't share details about our dates with Will and his team. They don't need to know my personal business."

"Yes, ma'am."

"And another thing…"

He wrapped his arm around her waist and pulled her toward him. "Are there a lot of rules? 'Cause you owe me a kiss."

She glanced around frantically. "Are you crazy? No kissing. Anybody could come along—"

He pressed his lips to hers before she could finish. It was quick—he'd rather not get her angry all over again—and only left him wanting more. "So, for dinner tonight," he began as if the kiss had never happened, "I thought we'd get some takeout and go back to the hotel and watch the race on TV."

"Takeout? Race?" She shook her head as if clearing her thoughts. "What hotel?"

"Ours. My room's kind of small. How's yours?"

"How do you know what hotel I'm staying in?"

He simply grinned.

"Dating a P.I. is going to strain my patience," she said with a dramatic eye roll.

"But it has its benefits. My undercover work is very refined."

IT WASN'T SO BAD, really, having a hot guy follow you around.

Well, two hot guys, Kylie thought, glancing at Will walking beside her toward pit road for qualifying.

Sean had hung around all day. He'd accompanied her and Will to the sponsor function, standing by patiently during the Q&A, even fetching her a bottle of water when she complained about the heat. Then, as they'd left the hospitality village, a gossip reporter had tracked them down, literally stepping into their path as they walked. Sean had given him one long, cold look, and the guy had stepped back, stammering with his request for comments about Alyssa's book and Hilton Branch's whereabouts. To which Sean had simply shook his head. The guy moved out of the way, and they headed on theirs.

Kylie wished she could work up some feminine indignation over the moment, but Sean simply had that type of presence and control.

Now, as they were nearing pit road, she noticed an unusual number of fans in the garage area for qualifying. When a group of them saw Will, they rushed over, shoving autograph books, ball caps and die-cast model cars toward him, slowing their progress. She'd been through the same scene many times, and, as long as they kept moving, they'd get where they needed to be eventually.

This group was more aggressive than the normal cluster of fans, though. It was odd, and she clenched her clipboard to her chest in defense. Maybe the heat had everybody on edge. Though she wore her self-sufficiency like a badge of honor, she again found herself grateful to have Sean so close.

"Will! Sign this!"

"Will! Look over here!"

The frenzied excitement of the fans was flattering to drivers, even though it could be distracting and overwhelming at times. With all the tabloid publicity that Will and his brother had had over the last few weeks, Kylie was all the more impressed with her driver's patience as he gave his rehearsed answers, ones Kylie had worked hard to create.

But when one ballsy fan pushed Kylie to get closer to him, Will stopped, his eyes firing as he turned.

Sean was between the fan and Will before Kylie could do little more than blink. "Mr. Branch is glad to sign your hat, sir, but you don't want to shove the lady."

Never taking his gaze off the fan, Sean took the hat, which he handed over his shoulder to Will, then he passed it back to the fan a moment later. His hard gaze swept the crowd, then he turned and, laying one hand on each of their backs, urged Kylie and Will to move forward again.

The group's aggressiveness died immediately. There were polite requests, smiles and thank-yous.

Kylie was amazed by the transformation, and the little effort Sean had exerted to make it happen.

The dichotomy of him was something she couldn't get her head around. He was a protector, but he could turn on the aggression at will, then flick it off like a switch and give her that charming smile.

In her experience, most law enforcement guys were one or the other. Most uniformed cops were protectors, loyal to their beat and their community. By contrast, the elite task force guys were coldly determined.

For the first time, Kylie realized that the best probably had both qualities. Matt had been all protector. He could barely work up a stern expression, even when Ryan had drawn on the walls with a permanent marker when he was two. He was a popular cop, with many loyal friends and colleagues, but he wouldn't have ever risen to the top of his field.

Sean could command armies if he so chose.

A guard stopped the crowd as they approached the pit wall. Only she, Will and Sean walked toward the black and gold race car.

"Smooth moves back there," Will commented, glancing at Sean.

"All part of the service," Sean said. "I appreciate you bringing me out here to see Kylie."

"Are you looking for a job?"

Sean shook his head. "I've got one, thanks. But if today's any indication, you might consider hiring some security."

"It's not usually that bad," Kylie said.

Will glanced at Kylie and smiled widely. "I have the feeling you'll be around a lot. I can pay you back in private plane rides."

Sean clapped him on the shoulder. "Deal."

Kylie shifted her glare between them. "When you two have finished with your male bonding and congratulating each other for that extra X chromosome, I'll remind you that I've done pretty well keeping Will on schedule and from being assaulted for a long time."

"It never hurts to have back up," Will said.

"Isn't she adorable when she's giving orders?" Sean asked Will.

Leaning back against his race car and crossing his arms over his broad chest, Will looked at her. "You know, she is. You're a lucky man."

Sean had the nerve to grin at her. "I know."

"Cut it out." Kylie glanced around. If anybody witnessed this ridiculous, humiliating exchange, she was going make life miserable for both of them.

"Did you ever notice that when she gets really mad, her eyes spark?" Will asked Sean as if she wasn't even there.

"They do. Like those wands we always light at New Year's."

"You—" she pointed at Will "—I'll make sure your next PR event is as a grocery store bag boy in Amish country, where hot, young girls won't even *think* about chasing after you."

She pointed at Sean. "And you, I'll tell everybody in the garage that although you look like a big, bad dude, you squeal like a girl when you see a cockroach."

They looked at each other, then at her. "That's just mean," they said together.

Smiling, Kylie blew on her nails. "That's right, boys. You remember who's in charge around here."

CHAPTER NINE

"THIS IS date number two, you know," Kylie said as she dug into her seafood chowder. "I'm expecting the white tablecloth Italian dinner soon."

Sean smiled slowly, but her heart rate picked up speed. "You won't be disappointed."

She glanced around her hotel room, which was small, but cozy. A mistake in reservations had gotten her two double beds instead of one king, but Sean had used that to his advantage, dragging out from against the wall the nightstand that sat between the beds. They each sat cross-legged on a mattress, their seafood feast between them.

Kylie had pulled her hair into a ponytail and changed into sweat pants and a T-shirt. She was gratefully wearing no shoes, and the NASCAR Nationwide Series race was underway on the TV, the volume turned low.

She'd forgotten how much fun it could be to just hang out, to not have awkward pauses in the conversation, to not have to worry about how she looked or wonder if her date was as concerned as she was by the lack of sparks, to be able to forget how her life had once been perfect—or as perfect as it could be.

With Sean, she didn't worry about any of those things. She simply enjoyed him. She looked across the makeshift table and into the eyes of a man who produced plenty of sparks and one who clearly found her attractive, even fascinating.

She still knew Sean was a big risk, but she could also see amazing rewards.

"So, what's the bounty-hunting business like?" she asked him.

His silvery blue eyes registered surprise. "You want to talk about my work?"

"All we've done all day is *do* my work, so yeah, let's focus on something else." She pursed her lips. "And, as I recall, the last time I brought up the subject of your work, you were a little vague."

"Ah…right." He took a sip of his wine. "Believe it or not, as I said before it's pretty routine most of the time—research, phone calls, questioning the right people. Most of the bond jumpers aren't dangerous. They're just scared. Or stupid."

"But the ones who *are* dangerous bring in a bigger bounty."

"Not always. It depends on who wants them and how badly. If a big bounty is put up by the government, then, yes, they're usually nasty dudes. I generally leave those to larger, more organized security firms. You need a big network of contacts to even find those guys, then a solid tactical group to bring them in."

Envisioning a team of black-suited warriors with

guns drawn and riot gear in place, she swallowed. "Have you ever been part of an operation like that?"

"Yes."

"But you don't want to talk about it."

His gaze moved toward the TV, but she didn't think he was seeing the race. "Not particularly, no."

She nodded in understanding. Plenty of memories weren't pleasant. She knew that better than anybody. "So when most of these guys see you on their doorstep, they come along quietly."

His expression brightened. "Pretty much."

"Like today with that rowdy group of fans. You have a presence."

"You think?"

She shoved his arm lightly. "You know you do."

"It's mostly an attitude. Something I worked hard to learn." When she angled her head, he continued, "I was a scrawny, clumsy kid."

Suddenly, she recalled the vulnerable expression in his eyes when he'd cut his hand on the tire iron.

"My brothers were bigger, stronger and faster," he went on. "I had asthma. But when I was in middle school I met a soccer coach who worked within the physical limits of my condition and helped me get stronger. Within two years of playing for him, and all evidence of my disease was gone. More than my physical strength, though, was the confidence he instilled in me. I knew I could do anything."

"No wonder you're so good with the boys," she said, clearly seeing the tender side of him she'd sensed from the first, the one he'd tried to hide. But the glimpse into his past didn't weaken him in her eyes; it increased his appeal and her longing to see more. And it was past time she showed him.

"When you know what it feels like to be weak, it makes being strong a responsibility, not a condition."

"The cute soccer coach is a philosopher?"

"Not exactly. It's something my karate master used to say." He rose and walked toward the desk. "You want some more wine?"

She held out her glass. "Sure." Once he'd given her a refill, she took a bracing sip. He returned to his seat, and she laid her hand over his, where it rested on the table. "I take it back. You're not cute."

The look in his eyes was somewhere between confused and insulted. "I'm not?"

"Nope. I bet you were cute as a kid. Probably even adorable—asthma and all." Smiling, she slid her hand up his arm. "Now, you're sexy. Dangerous. Alluring. Hot."

His gaze registered shock. "Are you coming on to me?"

"If you have to ask, I must not be doing it very well."

He set down his wineglass and moved around the table to sit beside her. "You're doing great. Keep going."

She slid her hand up his arm, across his shoulder to his chest, then paused over his heart. "Strong. You were always strong in here, I bet." Angling her head, she laid her lips over his.

She hadn't initiated a kiss with a man in a long, long time. She'd forgotten how lovely it could be to set the pace, to be the guide, to close her eyes and let desire roll over her naturally, without embarrassment or pretense. She could taste a hint of the wine and scent his earthy cologne, like smoky cedar or warmed whiskey on a cold night. Somehow she knew that ten years from now, she'd still associate that smell with Sean.

"We should probably be moving slower," she said when they parted, breathless.

He slid his lips across her jaw. "We should?"

Laying her hand in the center of his chest, she pushed herself back. "Yeah. I—" His heart was racing beneath her fingertips. Her own was doing the same. She was excited, but she was also scared. She didn't want to want him. "I'm going to splash some water on my face."

She practically ran to the bathroom. Closing the door, she leaned back against it, squeezed her eyes shut and tried to control her warring emotions.

Good grief, he probably thought she was a lunatic. A desperate widow, throwing herself at the young, hot stud. She was all over him one minute, then running from the room the next. Her face burned with humiliation. Was she crazy? She couldn't do this—date, kiss men in hotel rooms, get involved. She didn't know what she was doing, and when she went with impulse, she wound up cowering in the bathroom.

Cowering?

She opened her eyes. Kylie Palmer didn't cower. At least, she never had. She was a responsible adult. And she wasn't desperate. A little out of her element, maybe. Certainly out of practice with the moves of dating. She'd simply find her dignity and apologize. And if he didn't understand that she struggled with intimacy, then it was probably better to find out now.

After dabbing her face with water, she rolled her shoulders, then walked, head held high, out of the bathroom.

Sean was hovering outside the door. He laid his hands on her shoulders. "Are you okay? You turned sheet white. Are you sick?"

Wow. He really was great, wasn't he? If she had to pick a guy to make an idiot out of herself over, she'd chosen wisely. "I'm fine. But I'm sorry I jumped you, then chickened out. I didn't mean to tease—"

"Whoa." He pulled her against his chest, kissing the top of her head. "There was no jumping. There was kissing and touching. You're allowed to do that when you're on a date. Actually, you're allowed to jump, too, if you ever feel the need." He leaned back, smiling down at her. "And teasing can be a good thing." He slid his thumb down her cheek. "Anticipation is half the fun."

She raised her eyebrows. "Half?"

"Well, maybe a quarter." He brushed her hair back from her face. "There aren't rules here." He paused. "Well, maybe one—the only guy I want you jumping is me."

"I can live with that rule." She felt odd asking for the same in return, knowing he would agree. Even when he could have anyone. "Same goes."

"You got it." He pressed his lips gently, briefly to hers. "Second date, and I've already got an exclusive contract. I have to say, I'm good."

She licked her lips, imagined tasting his again. "This is moving forward pretty fast."

"I know. For me, too. We'll slow down a bit." He held her hand and led her down the short hall. He looked at the beds, then slid his gaze toward the single chair in front of the desk. "Hang on."

After a bit of rearranging, including folding a bed-spread and spreading it on the floor, then propping the pillows at the end of one bed, he'd made a make-shift lounge chair. He sat with his legs outstretched, and she sat between them, her back against his chest.

With the whole we're-on-a-*bed* pressure out of the way, she was able to relax and watch the race. They sipped wine and shared the single, but huge turtle brownie they'd brought from the seafood restaurant.

When chocolate sauce dripped on the corner of Sean's mouth, she dabbed it with her finger, then licked it off.

"Hey," he said with teasing insult, "where's mine?"

She dipped her finger into the remaining sauce on the plate, then pressed the pad against his lips. He sucked her finger into his mouth, and a jolt of desire rushed down her spine. The moment went from joking to intense in a heartbeat.

His gaze locked on hers. He wrapped her arm

around the back of his neck, bringing her face within inches of his. He covered her mouth with his, and desire spread all the way to her tingling toes. The warmth of his body and lips heated her blood, stole her breath.

"We're getting really good at that," he said when they separated.

She smiled, and for the first time realized she liked dating. "With a little more practice, we might get it perfect." She trailed her hand across his shoulder, feeling the ripple of muscles beneath. How often did he work out to get a body like that?

"Problem?" he asked.

Feeling her face heat, she flicked her gaze to his. "No way. Just wondering about your workout routine. It must be pretty…intense."

"Why would you think that?"

"Because of your super hot and sexy body."

His eyebrows climbed high on his forehead. "My what?"

She slid her fingers across his forearm. Yep, some pretty serious muscles there, too. "Not that I've seen it all, of course."

"We can fix that anytime."

She laughed. "I've got a pretty good imagination. Do you stay in shape now because you were sick as a kid?"

"Partly. It's also helpful on the job."

"I guess so." She walked her fingers up his chest, then ran them across his strong jaw. "Yep. Sexy and dangerous."

"Is that a good thing or not?"

She kissed him lightly, reveling in the fact that he was hers. For now, at least. "Definitely. And it fits your divergent personalities."

"My divergent...*what*?"

"You know, easygoing soccer coach of ten-year-olds by day, intense bad-guy chaser at night."

He looked amused and interested. "Is that right?"

"Sure. I find you pretty fascinating, actually."

"Do you?"

"On a purely academic level, of course."

"Of course."

She tucked her head beneath his chin. Snuggling was a wonderful thing. How had she forgotten how wonderful? "See, you've got opposing sides warring within you. You like being a free spirit, but you can't just be a surfer or—"

"Surfer?"

She patted his chest. "Sure. You've got the shake-it-dry hair, the relaxed California smile, the tan and did I mention the super hot bod?"

"I think that came up."

She lifted her head, twisting her neck around to look at him directly. Finding that uncomfortable, she slid off his lap and onto the blanket beneath them. Angling her body, she could see him better, lean against his side and tangle her legs with his. "Do you want to hear my personality assessment or not?"

"As long as my body continues to fascinate you, too."

"So where was I?"

"Opposing sides warring."

"Right." She, again, laid her head on his chest. "It's the surfer/warrior syndrome. On the surface you're easygoing, fun and casual, but underneath there's this simmering layer of strength and aggression."

She suppressed a shiver at her own warring sides. One wanted to remind her of the excitement; one reminded her of pain.

"Because you have the easygoing side," she continued, "you know how to control the aggression. And that's what makes you the best, the *very* best at your job."

She stared at the flickering images of the race on TV, but she focused on the past, both recent and distant. It was an odd place to find herself, but one she was sure she had to come to terms with in order to move forward.

Sean had pushed her to strive for sunlight when she'd been buried in grief.

"I'm not special, Kylie," he said quietly. "There are plenty of other guys out there, doing their job and risking much more."

She laid her hand along his jaw. "You're special to me. I've known a lot of cops, so I know how they think and act. Only the elite have what you have."

He was quiet for a long moment. "You've given this a lot of thought."

"Yeah, well, I think about you a lot."

"Same goes." His gaze dropped to her lips. "I think about touching you a lot," he added. "Sometimes your lips are all I can focus on." He brought her face to his, kissing her, which he did very well and could have continued to do for hours as far as Kylie was concerned. But he pulled back a few moments later, breathing hard, regret and desire filling his eyes. "I should go."

"Go?"

"Before I can't." He rose, then tugged her to her feet and gave her one more hard kiss. "What time do you have to be at the track in the morning?"

"Eight."

"Yikes," he said as they walked toward the door. "I have to get some work done, follow up with some leads and phone calls. Can I meet you there around noon?"

"Sure." Her body was still tingling from his touch. How was she going to let him leave? Was she ready to ask him to stay? How long did people date before they hopped into the sack these days?

Probably not long.

But she wasn't everybody, and she'd told him she wanted to take things slowly. Before she impulsively decided to press the accelerator, she needed to consider the consequences of her actions. Isn't that what she always told Ryan when he rushed into something and it turned out badly?

She had the feeling sleeping with Sean would not turn out badly.

He held on to her hand as he opened the door. "I won't see you for more than twelve hours."

They were like teenagers with their reluctance to part. It was all so cute and sappy. Was this one of the advantages to dating a younger man? A man who was much closer to his teenage years than she wanted to think about. "I could call you when I get to the track in the morning."

"Sounds nice. You'll be my wake-up call."

She rose up on her toes and pressed her lips briefly to his. "'Night, Coach."

He cocked his head. "Is that like an endearment?"

"Sure." She grinned. "*Honey* is taken, after all."

He backed away smiling, and after she closed the door, she leaned back against it. Dating was good. In fact, dating was pretty wonderful.

AFTER ROLLING AROUND for hours, tangling his sheets and unsuccessfully trying to get back to the dream he'd been having about Kylie, Sean finally gave up at 5:23 a.m.

He took another cold shower—his third since leaving her room the night before—dressed in jeans and a T-shirt, then settled at the desk to try to work. Answering his e-mail, he was intrigued by a message from an airline employee he knew who said she'd found a one-way reservation for Hilton Branch from Boston to Bermuda on the eleventh.

Branch, Boston, Bermuda. It was no doubt some goofy name game by Branch.

Sean had been through false leads like this before. Branch was eluding the FBI, the SEC and *him*. The man wasn't stupid. A one-way ticket bought in his own name was clearly a red herring.

Still, it wouldn't hurt to touch base with people

he knew in Boston. Or maybe he could feed this lead to the Feds, if they didn't have it already. Sending them running in circles wasn't going to win him the good citizen award, but if they got to Branch before he did, his big bounty—and the balloon payment on the company loan—was going to blow into the wind.

As he worked, he realized that he had to explain all this to Kylie soon. She wouldn't consider his connection to Branch just another case in a business she didn't like in the first place. She would consider it lying.

But he didn't want to spoil the peace. He didn't want to upset their relationship when it was still so new and fragile. He didn't want to lose her.

Was he wise or a fool to wait for the right moment?

When his cell phone rang, he jolted. Eight already?

"Sean, it's Kylie," she said when he answered.

"Morning." Sean leaned back in his chair with a smile, picturing her with her phone to her ear, her glossy dark hair brushing her cheeks. "It turns out I didn't need a wake-up call. I've been up for—"

"Somebody broke into Will's motor home," she said, her voice urgent. "Can you come out here?"

"I'm on my way." Heart pounding, he shut down his computer and grabbed his keys. "Are you guys okay?"

"We're fine. Whoever did it is gone. I'm sorry to bug you. I know you're working. I just…I don't want to call the police yet."

He ran down the stairs instead of waiting for the elevator. "Cops mean reports, and reports mean reporters."

She sighed in obvious relief. "Exactly."

"Hang on. I'll be right there."

He shoved away panic and drove with focused determination, even as his imagination supplied various horrific scenarios of Kylie walking in on an intruder. He reminded himself that hadn't happened. And Will was there. Will wasn't the typical size of a race car driver. His presence alone should be enough to scare off anybody stupid enough to mess with him or Kylie.

As he darted through the streets, questions assaulted him. Was there a possibility that this was connected to Hilton Branch? Could a giddy female fan have somehow talked her way past the guard in the drivers' and owners' lot? Could another driver have pulled a prank? Could it be that simple?

Maybe.

He pushed the rental car to its limits and reached the track in record time. He raced into the infield with no problem, thanks to his precious parking pass sitting in the front window. As he walked toward the lot, he noted the grandstands were deserted, the infield fairly quiet. Fans wouldn't start roaming around for a while yet. But the NASCAR Sprint Cup Series garage stalls were buzzing with race day activities.

A few reporters milled about. The rest were no doubt holed up in the media center, sipping coffee and hoping the budding stories would stay quiet until they managed to get their brain cells moving again.

The same guard from the day before was on duty at the entrance to the drivers' and owners' lot. He was in his early sixties and a retired cop, but his eyes were as sharp as they'd probably been when he was on the job. How had somebody who didn't belong gotten by him?

Maybe nobody had. Maybe Sean's visions of a deranged bank executive, burned by Hilton Branch, a crooked reporter after the story of the year or a rogue bounty hunter honing in on his territory were unfounded.

"Morning, Arthur," the guard said, stepping aside to allow him to pass through the gate.

Sean thanked heaven his instincts had urged him to make friends with the guy yesterday. "Morning, Frank. You been busy?"

"Pretty quiet this early, though I heard we had some excitement last night."

Wildly interested, but pretending casualness, Sean leaned against the fence. "No kidding."

"Some drunk idiot tried to talk his way past the guard and into the lot."

"Did he have infield credentials?"

"Nah. Musta wandered in from one of the campgrounds. I can't believe he got this far without getting stopped. Believe me, the boss man was fired up about it this morning."

"I bet. I guess you haven't seen anybody suspicious."

Frank crossed his arms over his chest. "Should I have?"

Too curious, Sean thought. Knowing he needed to back off, he shrugged. "I guess not. My girlfriend's Will Branch's PR rep, and she tells me it seems like a week doesn't go by that some fan— some *female* fan—isn't trying to get into the lot."

"Yeah, they try. But they don't get in. Not *this* lot, anyway." He shrugged. "Only people I've seen this morning are sponsors. One guy was here at seven, before I'd barely had my first friggin' cup of coffee. Claimed he had a meeting with Kent Grosso. I told him Grosso probably wasn't out of bed yet, and he wouldn't be happy to get woken up. The guy said he was expected. He had all the creds, so I let him go. I'm still waitin' to hear a complaint from Grosso."

Even as all his senses went on alert, Sean grinned. "Prank, I bet. Kent and Will have this crazy prank war going on. Was the guy mid-fifties, six feet, about two twenty, thinning light brown hair, full of himself?"

Frank's dark eyes registered surprise. "Four out of five. Had a full head of black hair. Looked like a wig to me, though." He shook his head. "Pranks, huh? Heat gets everybody squirrelly, especially these drivers. Wonder if that was the deal last night?"

"Could be." He started backing away. "I know you've got everything under control. You want some more coffee? A soda?"

"I'd love a soda. Thanks."

Sean grabbed the soda from a nearby vending machine for Frank, and then, after delivering it, moved quickly toward Will's motor home. How was the driver going to feel when Sean told him his father had been his B and E man?

Hilton Branch was smart, Sean reflected. Be yourself but get obvious fake hair. Then that's what people notice. Hilton Branch was a kabillionaire. People didn't consider him a regular fugitive, dangerous and a threat to the community. He was a rich, wily fugitive. He wasn't tacky. He would never be tacky enough to wear *fake hair*.

He rounded the corner of row three, his thoughts on his target and his motivation for breaking into his son's motor home. Since the break-in had been obvious to Kylie, there must be signs of forced entry or a search. Why? What did Branch want? Was he looking for something?

Slipping in to watch the race, Sean could understand. Breaking in made no sense.

Glancing up, he saw Kylie pacing *alone* beside Will's place, and his panic rushed back. He jogged toward and pulled her into his arms. "Where's Will?"

"He took Susan—the latest girlfriend—over to Bart's motor home. His brother," she explained unnecessarily. "They're twins. He races for PDQ Racing."

"He left you here alone?"

"I didn't tell him about the break-in, just that we needed to talk privately about something important. This lot is one of the most secure places at the track." Obviously realizing that wasn't true in this case, she added, "At least I thought it was secure. This is bad,

Sean. What if the other drivers find out? What if some crazy guy is targeting—"

"That's not what's happening."

She leaned back, looking up at him, her blue eyes focused, not alarmed. "How do you know?"

There were a lot of things he needed to say; there was much to explain. But later. The break-in had to be their focus. They both had jobs to do. He had a fugitive to bring in; she had a driver to protect. He only hoped they could both accomplish their goals without losing the shaky bond between them.

Fighting to stay calm, he stroked her back. "Just tell me what happened."

CHAPTER TEN

"WILL AND SUSAN GOT UP EARLY to go for a run," Kylie said, long past worrying about bruising her ego by calling for help. Break-ins were beyond her marketing scope, and she was extremely grateful someone she trusted, someone with an expertise in this area, had been nearby to come and take charge. "He'd told me yesterday they planned to do that. When I got here and no one answered my knocking, I figured they were probably still gone. I opened the door and walked inside."

"The door was unlocked?"

"No, but I know the code."

Sean nodded. "What did you see when you got inside?"

"The pillows from the sofa were on the floor. I thought that was weird, but then—" She felt her face heat. "Well, I figured Will and Susan had…slept together. So I turned toward the kitchen, hoping to find coffee. But I noticed opened cabinets, the counter littered with open packages of crackers, cheese and a cured sausage log on the chopping block. Everything looked fresh, not left over from the night before.

"I called Will's name, and when he didn't answer, I headed toward the bedroom. In there, clothes were scattered everywhere, drawers were pulled open, sheets were stripped off the bed. Will isn't a neat freak, but I've never seen his room like that." She gripped Sean's hand. "I've seen robbery crime scene photos and I suddenly realized that's what I was looking at. I rushed out of the motor home and called you."

"You did the right thing. Let me have a look."

He tucked her hand in his as they walked inside. After he walked around for a few minutes, he stopped in the ransacked bedroom. He still hadn't said a word.

"Who pauses to have a snack while he's trashing a place?" Kylie asked him, hoping to prod him into sharing his thoughts. She couldn't read him, couldn't tell if he was annoyed that she'd interrupted his work for something so simple, or if he was intrigued and trying to figure out the puzzle.

"It's certainly bizarre," he said.

"Should we call the police?"

"No way. It'll be on the news by noon if we do."

"But what if this guy, or whoever, comes back? What if he's dangerous?"

"I can change the security code on the door and add a motion sensor," he said absently, still seeming lost in thought. "Don't worry about Will. I'll protect him."

"That's not your—" She snapped her fingers as a memory from the day before jolted through her.

"That reporter from yesterday. The one who tried to block us from walking away from the hospitality village."

"It wasn't the reporter."

"It could be, though how could he know the security code? Maybe—" She suddenly realized his statement wasn't a guess or him just talking out loud. Her stomach clenched. Something weird was going on. "You know who broke in, don't you?"

"I do." His gaze met hers. "It was Hilton Branch."

"Oh, come on." Seeing the expression in his eyes and realizing he was serious, she whispered, "How do you know?"

"From talking to the guard at the gate."

A fugitive father was a PR nightmare for a NASCAR driver. She ought to know; she'd been dealing with it nonstop. Sean had to be wrong. "But everybody knows he's wanted by the police. The guard wouldn't have let him in."

"He was in disguise." He shrugged. "Sort of, anyway. He wouldn't have gotten by me, but I'm used to expecting the unexpected. And Hilton was bold and smart. It's just like him."

A chill raced down her spine. *Just like him? What do you know about Hilton Branch?*

"He's a fugitive, Kylie."

And you're a bounty hunter. A trace of suspicion wormed its way into her brain. Was Sean interested in finding Hilton? Was he going to use this opportunity to cash in? She supposed bounty hunters could go after anybody, but there had to be a bounty to collect in the first place, and Hilton Branch had the FBI after him. Why would they put up a bounty? Why would they need somebody like Sean when they had an army of dark-suited agents?

"He's big news in my business," Sean went on. "And you said it yourself—*everybody* knows about Branch. He's been all over the news for months."

They'd gotten past the barrier of his job—at least on a let's-just-have-fun, temporary dating level. But there was plenty she didn't know about him, plenty she wasn't sure she *wanted* to know. But, regardless of his interest in Hilton, she trusted Sean. His expertise was a blessing. She couldn't handle this crisis on her own.

"What are we going to tell Will?" she asked, biting her lip.

"The truth. His father broke in for a reason. And it wasn't a snack of cheese and sausage."

She nodded, then leaned back against the bedroom wall, closing her eyes. Like she'd done the night before in the bathroom, she wanted to shut out the pain and worry. Something wasn't right. She *just happened* to meet a bounty hunter who knew about Hilton Branch? She *just happened* to be crazy about him? She *just happened* to bring him to the track and introduce him to Hilton's son?

Her life was officially a mess.

And, for the first time in a long time, she didn't want to face it, didn't want to deal with whatever truth lurked behind Sean's eyes. She wanted her fun, sexy, temporary boyfriend back. She'd only had him for a day, and she wanted to enjoy him before life's complications ruined everything. She had no illusions that she'd hold Sean's attention for long, and she selfishly wanted her time. She *deserved* her time.

Sean cupped her cheek, his fingers warming her when ice threatened to coat her heart. "We'll get through this," he said gently, as if he'd guessed her thoughts.

"Sure we will," she said without any confidence. Laying her hands against his chest, she forced a smile. "How'd you sleep?"

"Terrible. I kept thinking about you."

"Yeah?"

He pressed his lips to hers, then trailed his mouth along her jaw. "I don't *stop* thinking about you."

She sighed against his cheek. "Same goes. And we'd better enjoy the time while we have it. Sunday night I turn back into a mom."

"Then we'd better make it count."

He closed his mouth over hers, and she curled her fingers into his T-shirt. She inhaled the now-familiar scent clinging to his skin. It had been a great many years since she'd put desire above common sense, since she'd craved a man's touch like a fire that needed oxygen to continue burning.

And there were moments, like now, when she wasn't sure she'd *ever* wanted someone the way she did Sean.

"Knock, knock," an amused voice said from behind her.

She jumped away from Sean as if an airhorn had

blasted in her ear. She valued her professionalism above everything except her family. She was making out *in her client's bedroom*. Ruling hormones were not a positive development in her life. At least not for her career.

"Will, I—"

"Not too often there's action in my bedroom that I'm not part of," he said, his eyes dancing with amusement as he leaned against the door frame, still dressed in his T-shirt and running shorts. "Looks like I missed all the fun."

From behind her, Sean laid his hands on her shoulders. "We didn't make the mess, Will," he said calmly. "You've had a break-in."

The smile fell away from Will's face. "A what?"

"I didn't want to upset yours and Susan's weekend," Kylie said, hoping her dignity would eventually return and that she'd be able to look Will in the face again without blushing. "This is the important thing I needed to talk to you about."

Will glanced around, no doubt taking in the messy room with new eyes. "Who? Why?"

"I need you to look around, check to see if anything's missing," Sean said.

"Should we call the police?" Will asked, looking frustrated and confused.

"I don't recommend it. Not yet. Look around, Will," he added in a quiet, but authoritative tone. "Kylie and I will wait in the other room. Then we'll talk."

Sean led her down the hall. They said nothing as

he stood by the door, staring out window, and she sat on the sofa, her hands clasped in her lap. Whatever personal needs and issues she and Sean had, they were put on hold. They needed to focus on Will.

What the hell is wrong with Hilton Branch?

As a parent, Kylie was appalled by his actions. But to skip town with the family's money and dignity, then suddenly appear in his son's life, jonesing for cheese, crackers and who knew what else was, well, despicable.

"Nothing's missing," Will said in a hollow voice a few minutes later when he appeared in the hall.

"You're sure?" Sean asked, his gaze focused on Will's face.

"I guess," Will said, clearly annoyed. "I don't take inventory every day."

"Sit down," Sean said, extending his hand toward the sofa.

Will's eyes lit with fury. "This is *my* home. You're here because I let you come. *You* sit down."

Calm and controlled, Sean crossed his arms over his chest, his feet braced hip-width apart. "You know I work in security, right?"

"Sure."

"Will you believe me when I say I'm really good at my job?"

Will visibly struggled with his temper. "Sure," he snarled.

"I can't drive 180 miles an hour like you do but this is my territory, okay?"

Saying nothing, clenching his hands by his side,

Will stalked to the sofa, then dropped down beside Kylie. "Fine."

Kylie reached over and grasped his hand. No matter how ticked off he was, how violated and out of control he felt, nothing could prepare him for knowing somebody he loved had made him feel that way.

"Why would your father come here?" Sean asked abruptly.

"I—" A thousand emotions swam into Will's eyes. "He wouldn't."

"But he did," Sean said.

"My father didn't do this."

"You have—or had—something he wants. What is it?"

"Money?" Will said, staring at the floor.

As Sean shook his head, Kylie studied Will, his hunched, defensive posture and uncharacteristic nerves, and realized he knew something. Why did she feel that she was the only one who'd arrived late to the movie?

"He took off with millions," Sean said. "He couldn't have run through it all already. Why would he risk coming here?"

After several minutes of silence, Will raised his head. "He sent me a box a few weeks ago."

"What kind of box?"

"A little metal lockbox. And don't ask me what was in it, because I never looked."

"Hell." Sean paced, pushing his hand through his hair. "He turned his back on you, on your brothers, sister and mother. He left all of you twisting in the wind while he lounged on the beach. What were you thinking, protecting him?"

Will's eyes flashed with determination. "I was thinking of protecting my mother. His note said the contents of the box would help her if I kept it safe for a couple of months. He apologized for taking off, said things just got out of control."

"You should have told the cops right off. Your father's on the run from at least two federal agencies. He won't last out there. He's too used to normal life, to luxury, even."

"I figured he'd put his will or something in there." He laid his head in his hands. "Obviously, he lied."

Kylie squeezed his arm and sent Sean a warning look. "Maybe he did. Don't feel guilty. Your father has made some terrible mistakes, but that doesn't mean you stop loving him or wanting to believe in him."

"No," Will said, glancing up at Sean. "You're right. He left us all high and dry. I should've done something. Something besides hide the box in the back of my closet. But Bart and I talked about it and decided to keep it quiet."

"You can do something now. Give me details. What did the box weigh?"

"Not much. The metal probably weighed more than whatever was in it."

"Size?"

"Maybe ten inches by five. A couple of inches thick."

"What about the postmark?" When Will hesitated, Sean added, "You had to have been curious."

"Miami." He stood abruptly, then headed toward the kitchen, where he took a bottle of water from the fridge and drank deeply. "You guys want anything?"

"We're fine," Kylie said, following him. Without comment, she straightened up the kitchen, returning the leftover sausage log and cheese to the fridge and loading the plate and knife into the dishwasher. "Are you going to be okay?"

Will leaned against the counter. "I need to talk to Bart, tell him what's happened."

"Do that," Sean said. "But don't tell anybody else. I'll contact somebody I know in the FBI and have him interview you and Bart in a few days. The last thing you want is the feds thinking of you two as accomplices or having the press getting a whiff of this mess."

Will nodded. "Fine."

Kylie knew better than most how families shattered irrevocably over one moment in time. All that was left to do was move forward—whether you wanted to or not. She started toward the living room. "We'll help you clean up."

"No," Will said, grabbing her arm and pulling her to a stop. "I'm sure you have a million things to do. I'll do it. It'll give me a chance to think."

She met his gaze. "Don't think too much. Focus on the race. Leave this to the experts."

"The race car is the only place I *don't* think about all this crap." Will pulled her against his side for a quick hug. "I'm fine. Don't worry, Kylie."

While Kylie crossed the room to get her bag and clipboard, she heard Sean's voice behind her.

"Don't beat yourself up," he said. "We all understand family loyalty."

"Even when one of them is a felon?" Will asked sarcastically.

THE RACE PASSED IN A BLUR of sound and speed. Several cars had special metallic paint schemes that gleamed off the bright lights around the track. Tension was thick in the air, as drivers fought for positions on the track and team members paced the pit boxes—everyone hoping to get into the all-important top twelve in championship points.

Since Bart won the race, Will finished second and both drivers got into the Chase, there were plenty of smiles and cheers to take precedence over the break-in that morning.

As Sean drove away from the rack, though, thoughts of his mission resurfaced.

"What do you think is in the box?"

Sean grinned at Kylie, her face dimly lit by the blue dashboard lights. The thrill of the hunt heated his blood. "Maybe diamonds."

She slapped his shoulder. "Oh, stop."

They'd stayed to help Will and his team celebrate, but now they were headed back to the hotel. Tomorrow Sean had to share Kylie again with her son, and as much as he enjoyed Ryan, he was equally enjoying his and Kylie's time alone. Being a parent must involve a lot of balancing.

"You constantly impress me. Today you juggled two print interviews, one TV interview, lunch with a sponsor, a crying jag from Will's girlfriend—"

"Weekend female guest," she corrected. "Will doesn't have much of an attention span when it comes to women."

"Probably why she was crying. Then you spent the race networking with the executives at Palco Foods."

"You never know when a connection leads to a sponsorship."

"I understand it all, but aren't you exhausted? Don't you want to prop your feet up? Sink into a bubble bath? Do you really want to talk about a metal box?"

"Yes, yes, yes and *yes*. Seriously, what do you think was important enough for Hilton to secretly mail?"

He decided not to call attention to the fact that she was fascinated with his case. First, because she didn't know it was his case, and second, because he wanted to enjoy her interest. She wasn't jumpy and worried about her brush with a federal fugitive, or nearly interrupting his B and E. She was *fascinated*.

And if she was fascinated by the hunt, she might eventually understand his constant need for it. She might understand *him*.

"Not diamonds," he said in response to her question about the box's contents. "Probably documents. Records, fake passports, personal accounting information. Swiss bank account numbers." Though he couldn't resist adding, "Maybe even money."

"He *mailed* a box of money?"

"He's done a lot riskier things."

"Good point." She glanced at him. "He'd mail money, but not diamonds?"

Even though he'd only been kidding, he considered the idea. Cash was more liquid, but more worth in diamonds could be mailed around, then carried on a person than the same amount in cash. And large cash deposits required a lot of bank paperwork. Which Hilton Branch would know only too well. "Could be either, I guess. Neither would weigh very much."

"Right. Will said the box was light." She tapped her finger against her lips. "It's so cool to speculate, huh? It's a puzzle. An adventure, even. Is this what your work's like all the time?"

"Not always, but sometimes."

He was certainly closer to his target today than he'd been yesterday. He couldn't wait to e-mail his brother and get him to start checking mailboxes in Miami. There was a chance Branch had rented one there, and he had to show ID to rent a box. Then again, it was just as likely he had a collection of fake IDs. In fact, he *had* to in order to get around this long without detection. And one of those IDs had gotten him past the guard at the drivers' and owners' lot gate.

How long had Branch been planning his escape? Months? Years? At some point, he had to have planned for the moment his scam would be revealed, and he'd have to disappear. He couldn't disappear with such efficiency on the fly.

Kylie slid her hand across his thigh. "Where'd you go?"

Her touch had his blood humming for an entirely different reason. "Just thinking about the possibilities."

"Are you going after him?" she asked quietly. "Are you going to try to find him now?"

Maybe she understood him more than he realized.

And though he was never one to avoid conflict when he knew he'd have to face it, he did now. He reverted back to the weak ten-year-old who was terrified he'd never overcome his obstacles. He laid his hand over hers and squeezed. "Let's drop Hilton Branch for now, okay?" Glancing at her, he smiled. "Tomorrow you turn into Super Mom again, and I want to enjoy the time I have you all to myself."

"I never said I was Super Mom," she said, and he was ridiculously grateful she let the subject of hunting Hilton Branch drop so easily. "But having you all to myself sounds pretty terrific."

He cast a quick look at her. "I'm available for anything."

Letting that promise drift in the air, they rode in silence for several minutes, her hand on his thigh, his hand covering hers. The road in front of them was dimly lit by the streetlights. They seemed alone in the dark. Intimately alone.

When he pulled into a parking space at the hotel and cut the engine, she angled her body toward him. "This is crazy," she said, her gaze flicking to his and holding. "We want each other. What are we waiting for?"

All the spit in his mouth dried to dust. "I have no idea."

"I'm nervous, I guess." She pulled her hand away and glanced out her window. "I haven't…um…slept with anybody since Matt died."

He'd guessed as much, but knowing and suspecting, he discovered, were two different things. There was some serious pressure in following behind the brave and martyred husband.

Now *he* was nervous.

He could move forward or retreat. Sean somehow knew the night was in his hands. She was waiting for some kind of signal, a push of encouragement. "I say we go upstairs and see what happens."

She whipped her head toward him. "Let's go."

Sean desperately tried to calm his nerves and his body as they walked across the parking lot, but his heart was pounding, his pulse racing. How did Will and the other competitors drive into a turn going 100 miles per hour and not have their hearts jump out of their chests?

He desperately needed their cool heads now.

He and Kylie held hands in the elevator and didn't look at each other. Did she feel the same tension, the same need as they watched the numbers light in slow succession? The anticipation of touching her, of holding her and being part of her, was like a fever.

"My room," he said the moment the doors slid

open, tugging her down the opposite end of the hall from hers. "The bed's bigger."

THE MOMENT Sean slammed the door behind them, they were breathless with laughter and in each other's arms. His body was like a sculpted work of art that Kylie longed to slow down and study, but Sean tumbled them onto the bed and she forgot everything except the way he made her feel.

Alive. Free. Sexy. Powerful.

She didn't consider the past or the future. She gave herself over to the present. Letting her needs take over was humbling and incredible. She focused on the intensity in his eyes, the emotions that moved, unspoken, between them as their skin glowed in the moonlight.

Later, when she tucked her head beneath his chin and felt his heart thrumming beneath her palm, she knew she'd found something special, something that, while fun, didn't feel temporary at all.

She'd waited so long to give herself to another man. Did she expect anything less than the hope and connection coursing through her heart and soul? She'd built a barrier around herself. When someone finally broke through those defenses, she was bound to fall hard.

A frisson of panic sang through her veins. One she tried to calm by tangling her fingers in Sean's hair and inhaling the scent of his cologne.

His hand stroked up and down her bare back. "Last night you said I was dangerous."

She lifted her head to stare at him. His eyes managed to reflect both satisfaction and concern. "I did?"

"You used it in context with me being sexy, so I'm probably taking things a step further." His hand slid up her back, then down. "Does the danger worry you? From my job, I mean?"

She didn't want to ruin the closeness, but, looking into his eyes, she had to be honest. "Yes."

He slid his hand across her cheek. "I'm careful, you know."

"I know." She wished she didn't have the urge to ask, but she did. Somehow, the darkness in the room and the silence, except for their breathing, made it easier. "Have you ever been shot?"

"Once. In the back of the thigh. When I first got my P.I. license, I was serving divorce papers and my servee wasn't ready to be single."

"In the *back* of your thigh? He shot you after you turned away?"

"Then he collapsed into a weeping puddle at my feet. It was a little hard to be angry."

"I think I could have managed it," Kylie said, pretty angry herself at somebody causing Sean pain. "What did you do?"

"Called 911 on my cell. And, as it happens, one of the paramedics was a hot blonde, who thought I was incredibly brave and stoic through the pain."

No telling how many women in his past had thought the same thing. No telling how many would in the future. Picturing women in his past made her smile, but thinking about the ones who'd come along after her wasn't nearly so pleasant.

She forced lightness into her tone. "You got the glory and the girl."

"And only a small scar. It was a pretty good deal."

"They said Matt was brave, too." Sean sucked in a surprised breath, and Kylie wished she could kick herself for the slip. "Sorry. I—" She wanted to crawl under the covers and hide. "This is why I don't date. I don't know what to say or how to act."

Sean urged her head up, cupping his hand beneath her chin. "You can say or do anything you want."

"I'm freaking you out, talking about my deceased husband."

"You're not. I told you before, I don't scare easy. I'm glad you feel comfortable enough to talk about him." He kissed her, then tucked her head back under his chin. "Do you want to tell me more?"

The only people she'd ever given details to about that day were her mother and Felicia. Ryan was still young enough that he'd been satisfied with vague information. She hadn't spoken aloud, in detail, for nearly four years.

"Matt had never been shot," she found herself saying. "The only time he'd ever fired his own weapon was at the range. A desperate kid came into a convenience store while Matt was buying a candy bar. He overreacted to the uniform. The bullet struck Matt in the neck. He bled out on the linoleum floor within seconds. At least he didn't suffer," she added in a whisper.

"What happened to the kid who killed him?"

"Life. Life in prison for a sixteen-year-old. I pleaded with the prosecutor not to seek the death penalty. Someday I hope to heal enough that I can send him a letter, to forgive him, so we can all move on."

"You will."

He kissed the top of her head, and her eyelids drooped. "Is it okay if I stay with you?" she murmured.

"You'd have to fight me to leave." He trailed his hand along her thigh. "But it is way too early to go to sleep."

His hand moved higher on her leg, and her eyes popped open. Suddenly, she wasn't tired anymore.

CHAPTER ELEVEN

"I'M GOING TO tell her tonight," Sean said to his brother, leaning in the frame of Jeremy's office doorway.

"About the Branch contract?"

"Yeah. Too much happened over the weekend in connection with the case." He had so many leads now, he'd had to prioritize which ones to chase down first. He'd made time the day before to take Kylie to the dojo for the karate class, and then they'd picked up take-out Chinese food for her family. They'd eaten at the kitchen table like a real family—even though Honey had sent him suspicious looks all during the meal.

"Before I could tell myself the case didn't have anything to do with her," he said to his brother. "Not telling her now is lying."

Jeremy leaned back in his desk chair and shrugged. "Lying is practically a job requirement in this business. And you always said you didn't discuss your work with anybody." He lifted his eyebrows. "Wisely so."

"I *have* to discuss it with her. I can't lie to her."

"I think it's a mistake. Look at all you've learned being around her."

"I'll still be around her. She'll just know why the information is so important to me."

His brother sighed. "Sit down, Sean."

"I'm on my way out. I'm taking her to Antonio's."

Jeremy angled his head. "I guess things are getting serious." He rose from his chair, sliding his hands into the pockets of his tan dress pants. "Sit down. This is the part where your annoying—but much more astute—older brother gives you relationship and career advice."

"As long as you make it fast," Sean said, crossing the room and dropping into one of the chairs in front of his desk.

"This is not an indictment on your lifestyle. You're a young, single guy. You have hot chicks lined up around the block, and you enjoy checking out the available options. Hell, my own wife fixes you up with her single friends every chance she gets. But your attention span isn't long." He shrugged. "Doesn't have to be. Mine wasn't either until I met Christine."

"Why do I think I'm not going to like the next part?"

"Don't tell her about Branch. You're so close to bringing him in. Don't trade one of the best retrievals of your career for a woman you've only been dating a couple of weeks." His gaze locked with Sean's. "Especially since, in another couple of weeks, you'll be bored with her."

A nasty curse word rose to Sean's lips, but he clenched his jaw instead of letting it escape. "No, I won't. I think I'm in love with her."

The disappointment in Jeremy's eyes was almost comical. "Ah, man, why'd you have to go and do that?"

"I have no idea." He stared at his hands. Hands that had touched Kylie and cuffed three jumpers in the last two weeks. Would she ever come to terms with that? "But it's there. And it complicates things."

"You *think*?"

Neither of them said anything for a few moments. Sean wondered if Jeremy was remembering when he met Christine and fell head over heels after the first date. Her wealthy father hadn't wanted her dating a regular guy from a working-class family, so they'd dated in secret. Then, when her father ultimately found out, they'd eloped in Vegas so he couldn't stop them from being together. Her father had cut Christine off without a cent, and their relationship was strained for years. Right up until the moment Patrick was born.

They'd had to fight for their relationship, just as Sean was about to have to do. But at least in Jeremy and Christine's case, they both wanted to fight. Sean was afraid his battle was all one-sided. Would he be able to convince Kylie that he hadn't used her to collect a bounty?

She'd trusted him enough to share his bed and her painful past. But the danger associated with his job was still a touchy subject. And the only way he'd been able to convince her to see him had been to tell her he *wasn't* serious about her—which was a really weird position for a woman to take, at least in his experience. He was her temporary boyfriend. Her hot affair.

As was usual with him, he was taking a calculated risk by telling her the truth about Hilton Branch. But all his instincts told him it was the right thing to do, and they hadn't failed him yet.

"So I have to tell her, don't I?" Sean asked finally.

"Hell, yeah, you have to tell her." Jeremy sighed—in disgust or resignation, he wasn't sure. "But if you lose Branch to the feds, I'm never going to let you forget it."

"The agents they put on his trail are too worried about messing up their manicures," Sean said as he rose. "I'm not letting a couple of pretty boys like them outmaneuver me."

"Any more word on the box?"

"Nothing definite. I'm checking pawn shops and jewelry brokers now to see if anybody matching Branch's description has sold any gems."

"The diamond theory," Jeremy said, clearly skeptical.

Sean's teasing comment to Kylie had become a full-fledged possibility. First, because it was smart for a man on the run like Branch. Second, because he was sure Branch would like the excitement of it, the romance and adventure. "More likely it's bank records or cash, but I'm not ruling out anything."

"What about the flight to Boston?"

"Ticket was never claimed."

"You figured that was a wild-goose chase from the beginning."

"Nice to know my instincts are still in working order." He hoped a little luck would tip the scales in his favor tonight. "I need to get going." He headed toward the door.

"Eat first," Jeremy advised. "A little wine wouldn't hurt, either."

"Thanks." Sean smiled slightly. "I'll keep that in mind." Just before he reached the door, he turned. "If I can't convince my own brother I'm serious about her, how am I going to convince her?"

"You've convinced me," Jeremy said.

Sean wondered if Kylie would be so agreeable. Maybe she'd look into his eyes, see the pathetically obvious feelings he had for her, and realize he'd never, ever hurt her or betray her in any way.

But he wasn't counting on it.

"I DON'T THINK this is a good idea," Honey began as she walked into Kylie's bedroom.

Kylie turned away from the mirror, where she'd been trying to decide if she should have gone for the traditional little black dress instead of the slinky red one she'd bought on her lunch hour. "What's not a good idea?"

"Going out with Sean. *Again.*"

Kylie planted her hands on her hips and stared at her mother. "What are you talking about? You're the one who encouraged me to go out with him in the first place."

"For one night of fun. Maybe a weekend. You can't have a *relationship* with him."

"I'm not having a relationship. I'm having a fling, Mom. You have them all the time."

Her mother rolled her eyes. "You've never had a fling in your life, Kylie Elizabeth Richardson Palmer. You dated one boy all through high school. Another one almost all the way through college. You met the last one your senior year and married him."

True as all of that was, she was hoping her future could be different. Since meeting Sean, she'd decided she missed out on a lot of fun in her younger years. "Well, I'm having one now."

She liked sneaking off to Sean's apartment for lunch, and sex—which she'd done on Monday. She liked making out in Sean's jeep—which she'd done last night. She liked the attention he lavished on her, and the envious looks from other women, who clearly were wondering, "*How'd* she *land a guy like* him*?*"

"And what would be wrong with having a relationship with Sean if I wanted one anyway?" she asked her mother, throwing her an annoyed look. "Aren't you the one who's paranoid I'm going to end up bitter and alone?"

"We already discussed this. He's too young for you."

"No, he's not." In fact, Sean's age didn't bother her in the least anymore. Was that because she had an issue with his job that overrode those concerns, or because she'd decided dating a younger man simply added to the fun? Either way, she was comfortable with her decision. "He's perfect. Especially for a fling."

"Okay. Fine. But then you have another, bigger problem."

"Do I?" She turned back to the mirror and wondered if she should add red lipstick to match the dress. "What's that?"

"*He's* not having a fling."

"Now you've really lost me. He was here last night. You saw him."

"Men having a fling do *not* bring Chinese takeout to their flingee's widowed mother and young son. Even if the widowed mother is amazingly attractive."

Kylie's jaw dropped. She *had* to get her hands on this dating rule book her mother seemed to know by heart. It was wildly enlightening stuff.

"They meet them at nightclubs or bars on the other side of town," Honey continued. "They sneak off for noon appointments that involve motel rooms rented by the hour."

It was good to know she was doing this at least partially right. She crossed her arms over her chest. "How do you know we're not doing all that stuff, too?"

That seemed to give her pause. Either she decided that wasn't possible or she didn't want to think about her daughter doing heaven knew what in a motel in the middle of the day, because she calmly answered, "Because of the way he looks at you."

"How does he look at me?"

"Like you're the center of his world."

"And that's a *bad* thing?"

"Men having flings do not look—"

"At the flingee as if she's the center of his world," Kylie finished for her. "Should I be taking notes on all these rules?"

"Don't be flip with me, Kylie Elizabeth."

"That's twice you've used my middle name. I must really be in trouble."

Honey perched on a corner of the bed. "I'm concerned. I want you to make the right choices, to be happy again."

Kylie sat next to her. "I am. Sean makes me happy. For now, isn't that enough?"

Honey's gaze searched hers. Finally, she nodded. "I guess it is."

A soccer ball tucked under his arm, Ryan raced into the room and dove onto the bed, nearly bouncing her and Honey off. "Why do I have to stay home again?"

Deciding she could only handle one conflict at a time, Kylie didn't remind her son—again—not to jump on the bed. "We were all together last night. Tonight is for grown-ups only."

Ryan rolled his eyes. "Sounds boring."

"To you, it probably would be. I'll bring you home some dessert."

Ryan's eyes lit up. "Like one of those brownies with chocolate sauce?"

"If they have it."

Rolling onto his back and tossing the ball up, then catching it, he asked, "Has Coach kissed you yet?"

Kylie exchanged a panicked look with Honey, who was amused. A mother's revenge, having to watch her child answer the same dicey questions she'd once had to deal with. "That's private between me and Coach."

"I hope he hasn't," Ryan said.

Why were flings for moms so much more complicated? Was she scarring her child for life? She'd been clinging to the hope that since this relationship wasn't going to last long, and Ryan and Sean were friends first, they'd still be friends afterward. And wasn't it healthy for her son to see her date? Even moms were entitled to a little romance and excitement, weren't they? "Why do you hope he hasn't?"

"'Cause in the movies, the guy always gets this goofy look on his face before he kisses the girl. Coach is too cool to look like that."

Romance in the mind of a ten-year-old male.

The doorbell rang, and Ryan ran from the room. "I'll get it!"

Kylie took one last look in the mirror, and Honey rose with her, sliding her arm around her waist. "That's certainly a flingworthy dress," her mother said with a twinkle in her eye.

"I guess it is." And she was glad she'd chosen it over the black one.

She grabbed her purse and headed downstairs. Sean and Ryan were in the foyer. Her son was showing her date how he could spin the soccer ball on top of his finger, the way Sean had done the previous night for what seemed like endless minutes. After the Chinese food, they'd spent more than an hour in the backyard practicing, and clearly the training had paid off.

She could hear her mother now. *Men having a fling do not play soccer with their flingee's young son.* Well, just because a man was kind, considerate and generous didn't mean he didn't know how to have a proper fling. She wished she could have zinged Honey with that one earlier.

And what was all that craziness about the center of his world?

When she reached the foyer, Sean grasped her hand and pulled her to his side. He kissed her cheek. "Hi, Kylie."

She met his gaze and flushed from the heat in his eyes. "Hi, Coach."

The ball hit the floor, bouncing until Ryan grabbed it. "Kissing. Yuck. I'm outta here." He ran down the hall. He stopped just before he rounded the corner to the kitchen. "Make sure you bring her home on time, Coach," he said sternly, then darted out of sight, laughing like crazy.

Sean smiled at her mother. "Hi, Honey. Thanks for watching Ryan for us tonight."

Honey smiled warmly in return; none of the worry she had about Sean showed. "He figures it'll be easier to get me to let him stay up late."

"Ah ha."

"I hear you're going to New Hampshire with Kylie and Ryan."

"Yeah. A buddy of mine has a camper he's letting me use. Ryan and I can hang out and roast marshmallows while Kylie works."

"I'm grateful," Honey said. "I'll have a weekend all alone." She glanced at Kylie. "Whatever will I do?"

Knowing her mother, it would be something extremely flingworthy. "I'm sure you can entertain yourself for a few days," Kylie said soberly.

She tracked her son down in the kitchen and kissed the top of his head. Then she and Sean headed out to his jeep, holding hands as they walked down the sidewalk. And though he said nothing, Kylie could feel the tension coiled in his body. She started to ask him if everything was okay, but she got distracted by his profile. She always wanted to stroke the perfect line of his sculpted jaw.

The moment they were inside the jeep, he leaned over and kissed her, long and slow. "Wow," he said when he pulled back. "You look…" His gaze drifted over her face, then down her body. "Wow."

She curled her hands into self-conscious fists beside her. Flings came with great compliments. "Thanks."

"You do amazing things for a black and white uniform, but I gotta say having you off duty is even better."

"I don't have a uniform."

"Sure you do. All the reps do. White shirt, black or

khaki pants. Discrete sponsor logo over the left pocket."

"I'm not that predictable."

He glanced at her, his gaze again moving over her red dress. "You certainly aren't."

At the restaurant, they were shown to a corner table, set with flickering candles and sparkling crystal on a white linen tablecloth. Just as Sean had promised. Over wine and dinner, they talked about their families and growing up. Because of their age difference, they had slightly different tastes in music and world event memories, but there were plenty of overlapping areas. They agreed on most political hot buttons, the importance of faith and the desire to someday have a grand home on the lake, similar to Honey's.

As the waiter cleared away their plates, Kylie studied Sean across the table. Was that the center-of-his-world look her mother was so worried about? Surely not. That was just Sean. It was the way he always looked at her. He was attracted to her, interested in her. Why was his focus a bad thing? Did it have to mean something earth-shattering?

Of course not. Chemistry. They simply had great chemistry.

Perfect for a fling.

"Dinner was great," she said to distract herself from deep thoughts. "The Italian restaurant date lived up to its billing."

"I'm glad." He covered her hand with his. "You want to take a walk around the park?"

"I hear couples go on that path to make out."

He grinned. "Do they?"

Returning his smile, she stood. "Let's go."

He paid the bill, and they walked outside. Antonio's restaurant was located at the edge of a small, lakeside state park. During the day, the area was filled with joggers and fishermen. At night, couples took advantage of the dimly lit paths and alcoves of tree-shaded benches for romantic interludes and even proposals.

The marketing executive in Kylie had always found Antonio's business plan pretty flawless.

"My son is concerned we're kissing," she said as they turned into the park.

"From his reaction earlier, I kind of figured that. Are you worried about him? Should I talk to him this weekend?"

"Not worried like that. He just thinks you're too cool to be a kisser."

He laughed. "From a ten-year-old, that's *got* to be a compliment."

They walked a little further, saying nothing, then Sean said the dreaded words. "We need to talk."

"From your reaction earlier, I kind of figured that." She forced a smile at her cleverness, repeating his words back to him. "What's wrong?"

He gave her an odd look. "Why do you think something's wrong?"

"When we walked out of the house earlier, I could feel the tension in your hands."

"That was because I was trying to keep from attacking you in the driveway." He glanced at her, but his eyes were shadowed, and she couldn't tell what he was thinking. "This is different."

Her stomach fluttered. Is this where the fling ended? She knew he'd move on eventually, but she'd hoped for a little more time. "Well, let's find a bench and get on with it."

Thankfully, they found one quickly before Kylie's nerves could get to the point that the shaking in her stomach got out of control.

Sean drew a deep breath, then released it. "I'm not sending a federal agent to talk to Will and Bart about the break-in."

"I—" This was work-related? She stared at him. *No way.* This was personal. "Okay," she said finally, confused. "Why not?"

"I've been hired to find Hilton Branch."

She closed her eyes in relief. "I'm sure that'll be a comfort to his family. Will knows you. He's worried his father will get killed if he resists being brought in by the FBI. And after that break-in, I'm not surprised the family hired you."

"Not after the break-in," he said quietly, watching her closely. "Before. Long before."

The fluttering returned to her stomach, as if a dozen angry bees were caught inside her. "How long before?"

"Since the beginning of August. Several bank investors got together and hired me because the feds obviously couldn't catch him. They want their money back and Branch in jail. It's where he belongs, of course, and after meeting Will and Bart, I'm only more determined to bring him in. They deserve some closure and a chance to confront their father."

Since the beginning of August, since the beginning of August...

The angry bees climbed to her throat, and the blood drained from her head. Pretty sure she was going to pass out, she grabbed the metal arm of the bench. "Did you know about me? About who I was the rep for when we met?"

"I did."

She jumped to her feet and would have stormed away if Sean hadn't grabbed her arm. "Let go," she said coldly, glaring at him.

"I need to explain."

"I've heard enough, thanks." She yanked her arm away, but she found suddenly she wasn't through having *her* say. "Nice work, really. Clever. Efficient. Bold. Flirt with the lonely widow, get her to introduce you to NASCAR's elite. Charm her enough to have her trust you with her client. And if there's a side benefit of getting her in the sack, all the better."

The muscle in his cheek pulsed. His eyes lit with anger. "That's what you think of me? You think I'd seduce information out of you to solve a case?"

"Yes."

He flinched as if she'd hit him. For a moment, she wondered if she'd said too much, but the betrayal and humiliation rolling off her was too strong to contain. She couldn't believe she'd been so easily taken in by a few compliments, hot kisses and pretended efforts at kindness.

"I *didn't* use you," he said, his voice strained but calm. "I asked you out because I was attracted to you. I'm dating you because I'm crazy about you. None of that has anything to do with bringing in Hilton Branch."

"Do I look that gullible?"

"I never, for one moment, considered you gullible," he said with quiet, barely contained resentment. "But you are stubborn." He stood, sliding his hands into his pockets. "Incredibly stubborn. Are you really going to look back on the last few weeks and tell me you think I was faking everything between us? That I spent my nights twisting my imaginary handlebar mustache and wondering how much fun it would be to tie you to the train tracks and hear you scream?"

She shook her head. Sean wasn't evil. He was a clever manipulator. That was really worse. At least evil was obvious. "Why tell me now?" she asked, her tone unforgiving. "In another few minutes, you could have had me sighing your name. My hot red dress could have wound up in a pool of satin on the floor of your apartment."

"I didn't like the secret hanging between us."

"So your motives were pure." Crossing her arms over her chest, she shook her head. *"Please."*

He returned her glare with one of his own, leaving her to wonder what he had to be so angry about. *She* was the injured party here. Didn't he even have the *decency* to look guilty?

"My work often involves secrets," he said. "I don't discuss specifics of my cases with *anybody* except my brothers. But after last weekend's break-in, your curiosity in the case and questions about it, I couldn't *not* tell you. I couldn't lie to you."

"You lied to me from the beginning! You've been lying since the moment we met. First the bounty hunting and now this…*who* you were hunting." She couldn't comprehend the betrayal. She recalled thinking Sean knew a lot about the Branch case and wondering why the government would hire him to chase down their fugitive when they had their own agents. Why hadn't the possibility of somebody else hiring him occurred to her?

You were too busy throwing yourself at the sexy, hot bounty hunter and getting naked in hotel rooms to think properly. That's why.

"Take me home," she said, turning away from him. "I can't look at you anymore."

I can't face myself and how stupid I've been.

"We need to talk about this. Please let me explain."

She shook her head.

"Maybe I went about things the wrong way," he continued, ignoring her refusal. "Maybe I should have told you sooner. But if I had, would you have gone out with me at all?"

"No."

He said nothing for a long moment. "My business needs this bounty. I didn't mean to hurt you, and I *didn't* use you."

She whirled to face him, refusing to let the softness in his voice sway her. "I don't give a *damn* about your bounty."

"Or me."

She said nothing.

Finally, he nodded. "I'll take you home."

She walked ahead of him out of the park and to the jeep. He was careful not to touch her; she was careful not to look at him.

By the time they were on the road, a touch of sorrow and regret had worked its way through her fury. Memories washed over her. Of Sean leaning toward her earlier, the heat and appreciation in his eyes before he'd kissed her. Of him gently tucking Ryan into bed. Of him making an impromptu sofa on the floor of her hotel room in Richmond. Of him and Ryan concentrating on some complicated soccer kick in the backyard.

Don't think about it.

It meant nothing. That was over. It was all over.

"Don't walk me to the door," she said when they pulled into her driveway.

"Fine." He shoved the jeep into Park, then snagged her arm as she tried to get out. His gaze was fierce as it met hers. "I *never* used you, Kylie. Once you calm down, remember I got to the race track all by myself last weekend."

The track. Sean and Ryan's weekend camping. What in the world was she supposed to do about that? Disappoint her son because his friend had crushed her?

She wanted to collapse into a heap and cry. Instead, she forced out an order. "Don't tell Ryan anything about this."

"Why would I?"

Vague answers like that were what had gotten her into this mess in the first place. In hindsight, she could see how easily he'd snowed her. "I want yes and no answers from you."

He clenched the steering wheel until his knuckles turned white. "I won't tell Ryan anything about me looking for Hilton Branch. What are we going to do about camping this weekend? I promised him."

He might not really want her, but he at least thought of Ryan before himself. "We're going to pretend everything is fine. That should be easy for you."

"But hard for you, since you won't even look at me."

She turned her head, deliberately looking him dead in the eye and fighting back the tears that threatened to fall. "After this weekend, I'll explain we're not dating anymore."

"That's it? We're over."

"You can be with Ryan, but not me. I need my job, and if the Branches and my boss find out who you are, they'll never trust me again. That dream of owning a lake house you so cavalierly agreed with is real for me. I need this job to save for a place for Ryan and me. You won't jeopardize my plans."

"That dream is real for me, too."

"I don't believe you." She opened the door and slid out. "I can't. Not anymore."

She ran into the house and prayed he didn't follow her and see the tears rolling down her face.

CHAPTER TWELVE

SHE HAD A RIGHT to be angry, Sean reminded himself for the four hundredth time.

It was Friday afternoon. Qualifying had just gotten underway, and while he was waiting for Ryan to show up, he sat at the small folding table he'd set up outside his borrowed camper in the speedway campground at New Hampshire and told himself—again—that he'd never expected she wouldn't be angry.

But he hadn't expected the hurtful things she'd accused him of. He hadn't expected the complete lack of trust. What had he done to deserve *that*? When had he been so horrible that he'd deserved *I can't look at you anymore*?

When the despair of those unfair accusations rushed over him, he hoarded his injured ego and wounded heart, reminding himself that she'd never taken him seriously in the first place. He'd been committed to their relationship. He'd been the one pursuing, the one who needed not just physical intimacy, but the whole relationship package. How could *she* feel so betrayed when she'd never wanted him beyond a casual fling?

She trusted him with Ryan, with her *child*. But refused to believe him about his case. Refused to let him past the thick wall around her heart. Stubborn. She was unreasonably stubborn.

He glanced at his watch. Ryan would be here any minute. He needed to put all this away, so he could enjoy him. Were their days together numbered? For all Kylie's promises that he and Ryan could remain friends, he was afraid she wouldn't let that happen. Not if she steadfastly refused to believe he hadn't used her.

He probably should have told her he loved her.

Because sometime between her accusing him of seducing her to earn his bounty and the hurtful sheen of tears in her eyes when she'd jumped out of the jeep, he'd realized he certainly did. Completely. Forever.

And *not* hopelessly, he thought, bracing his elbows on his knees as he stared at the ground.

He refused to believe she'd dismissed the life and heat between them like a weed choking a flower into dust. He refused to believe he couldn't find a way to reach her. There *had* to be a way to make her believe him. They just had to get past the anger and hurt. For him as much as her.

He certainly couldn't go through the rest of his nights like the last two, where he'd wandered aimlessly around his apartment—or the camper, in last night's case—cursing her with one breath and then with the next considering an appearance on her doorstep to beg her forgiveness. He wanted to shake sense into her almost as much as he wanted to hold her again.

"Hey, Coach!" Ryan said.

Sean jerked his head up to see Ryan rushing toward him, a gold and black model race car clutched in his hands. The excitement on his face brought a lump to his throat. He loved the boy as much as he did Kylie. How was he supposed to let them go?

He couldn't.

There has to be a way.

He rose from his chair. "What do you have there, buddy?"

"An RC car. Wanna see?"

Before Sean could answer, Ryan had plopped the model on the ground and was using the remote control in his hand to make the car scoot over the grass and dirt around the camper. "Cool, huh? It's a replica of Will's car he's going to run at Homestead. It's limited edition, and they don't even go on sale for two more weeks."

"Incredible," Sean said, his gaze flicking from the car to Kylie.

She physically stood only a few feet away, but they were miles apart in every other respect. There was no warmth in her gaze. She kept her eyes focused on a spot over his shoulder. "I need to talk to you privately for a minute," she said, her tone emotionless.

"Okay. Let me talk to your mom, Ryan, then we'll get started on our cookout."

Ryan didn't look away from his car. "Sure."

Sean followed Kylie into the camper. With all the lots around them filled, there wasn't a lot of privacy. But the people on either side of his spot had thankfully gone into the stands to watch qualifying, so at least they wouldn't be overheard.

"Will would like to talk to you about the break-in," she said in a low voice, her gaze flicking toward the windows, beyond which Ryan played with his car. "He and Bart think they should call the police. I've convinced Will to hold off for the moment, but he wants to hear your thoughts about the investigation into his father's disappearance."

"I'd be glad to talk to him," he said, wishing he'd thought to do so before now. Just because he and Kylie were having problems didn't mean he should abandon Will.

"I'd appreciate it if you wouldn't tell him about you being hired to find his father."

"I think it's time I do. I should have told him last weekend, but—"

"I'm asking you *not* to tell him," she said through clenched teeth. "You owe me that."

His temper, barely contained since Wednesday night, fired anew. "But that's not the truth. You *want* me to lie?"

She glared at him. "You can tell him after you bring in Hilton. If you tell him now, it'll look like I helped you deceive everybody."

"I haven't deceived anybody."

"Oh, really?" She angled her head as if confused, but her eyes were glittering with resentment. "You've told everybody in the garage who you are and what you're doing when you questioned them about Hilton?"

Hell. She knew he hadn't. His job required secrets. But he was an investigator, not a gossip.

He bowed his head, finally understanding her need to not look at him. Looking into her eyes when she held him in such contempt was unbearably painful. She'd told him that she didn't want to ruin his and Ryan's friendship, and that meant they'd have to find a way to at least be cordial to each other.

But how could he do that when he looked at her and his heart went crazy? When he missed her so much that he could hardly keep himself upright, much less concentrate on the case and bounty that used to be so vital?

"I won't tell Will," he finally said. And Will probably wouldn't forgive him for keeping his profession a secret. Another relationship ruined. What was one more? "The only person I cared about telling was you."

Turning away, she said nothing.

He let his anger simmer for a good twenty seconds before the question burst from him. "If it's convenient for me to lie *for* you, why are you so upset that I lied *to* you?" He paused when she stopped. "Kind of a double standard, don't you think?"

She looked at him over her shoulder, her eyes were empty of expression. "Please make sure Ryan is in bed before midnight."

"Yeah, sure."

She left, flipping the camper door closed behind her with a decisive snap.

Great. Now he was his girlfriend's son's babysitter.

Or was she his ex-girlfriend, now that she was barely speaking to him? Or was she ever really his girlfriend?

Despite his screwed-up love life and the possibility of his career crashing and burning, he forced his problems to the side and concentrated on Ryan. The kid had had plenty of hard knocks in his life, but he was dealing with them much more gracefully than Sean himself.

And men, as Kylie had told him, were driven by food, so they dealt with their issues by eating.

They made burgers and ate salad—part of Sean's ridiculous plan to prove to Kylie that he could have fun and still think of Ryan's nutritional balance. They alternated between watching qualifying on the TV inside the camper and going outside to hear it live. Later, after the sun set, they roasted marshmallows and made s'mores, which Ryan was an expert at doing, thanks to his many camping trips with Honey.

They eventually settled on the sofa and watched one of the pre-Mom-approved movies Kylie had sent with Ryan. Sean enjoyed their time together and was sure Ryan did, too, even more so when Sean didn't focus on morose thoughts such as, *She's the love of my life, and she hates me.*

"Why's my mom mad at you?" Ryan asked as the credits rolled on the movie.

A question like that couldn't lead anywhere positive, and Sean struggled between the truth and the convenient answer—apparently a theme in his life lately. "We argued," he said vaguely.

"About me?"

Sean started to shake his head, but Ryan jumped to his feet and rushed on. "You don't want to take my mom to dinner anymore because of me! Jimmy Anderson's mom cries all the time because her boyfriend didn't want kids, and his dad left them when he was five. He acts like he doesn't care about a dad, but I know he does. I don't know if I want another dad, but my mom always smiled when you were around, and now she doesn't."

Why were kids so often the victims of lousy adult decisions? Sean swallowed the lump in his throat with a great deal of effort. "Sit down, Ryan."

Ryan shook his head.

Stubborn, just like his mom.

As much as Sean wanted to hug Ryan against his side, he didn't move. His future hung in the balance with this conversation every bit as much as it did with convincing Kylie he wasn't a lying jerk, using her for his own gain.

"We didn't argue over you," he said, trying to stay calm, to find the right words and not say anything that would infuriate Kylie any further or have Ryan blaming himself. "If you ever decide you do want another dad, any man, including me, would be proud to have you. We disagreed about my job."

Ryan rolled his eyes. "Installing security alarms? What's the big whoop about that?"

Oh, man. He'd promised Kylie he wouldn't

discuss the dangers of his job. "I travel a lot," he said, then quickly decided that was enough information on bounty hunting for now. The real, deeper issue was something he actually felt more comfortable discussing. "And your mom loved your dad very much. She's still sad that he's not with you guys anymore."

Those deep blue Kylie-like eyes blinked back sudden tears. "I am, too." He shuffled his feet and stared at the floor. "Sometimes."

"It's okay to be sad. But I bet your dad would want you to be happy most of the time."

"Yeah. I guess."

"You're mom's trying to be happy."

Ryan's head jerked up. "For me?"

"And for herself."

Ryan said nothing for several long moments, and sweat rolled down Sean's back. Experience with nieces and nephews was nothing compared to the approval of the child you'd like to tuck in every night, even though you had absolutely no right to.

"You made her cry," Ryan said fiercely.

I did? Sean tried not to picture the tears he'd seen in Kylie's eyes actually falling, but failed miserably. "I said I was sorry," he said, knowing that was a lousy answer.

Ryan fisted his small hands at his sides. "Say it again."

So simple. So true.

Sean nearly laughed over the childish advice, but it was too good. Kylie didn't trust him. He had to prove himself trustworthy. He had to apologize. Again. And again. And as often as it took for her to believe him.

Was this all just that easy?

Well, not *easy*, but *basic*.

Words meant nothing. In his business, suspects lied to get themselves out of everything. Actions were what mattered. If you made a mistake, what were you going to *do* about fixing it?

"You're right," he said, rising from the sofa. He paced. Considered. Planned. These were things he normally excelled at doing, but tonight his thoughts were jumbled, disjointed. Strategy was much more difficult when everything you wanted and dreamed about was on the line.

"What are you going to do?" Ryan asked, sounding more curious than angry now.

He stopped pacing and dropped onto the sofa. "I have no idea."

Ryan sat beside him and patted his knee. "You're not very good at this dating stuff, are you?"

Sean stared at him. Then he started laughing. Though it sounded and felt a little strange at first, he quickly grew used to the lightness in his chest. It was familiar and comforting. Despite his Irish ancestry, he wasn't cut out to brood for long.

He hugged Ryan to his side. "Thanks, buddy."

"I'm never dating. Dating makes cool guys turn into weirdos."

"I wouldn't be too sure about that. The right brunette comes along, she'll knock you between your eyes and you'll be a goner." Sean certainly knew he was.

"I make Mom a card sometimes. You know, when she's sad or mad at me."

"This is going to take more than a card, I'm afraid."

"What about flowers? Honey always gets this big smile on her face when one of the captains sends her flowers."

"Captains?"

"At the yacht club. All the old guys hang out and play cards or go boating." He grinned widely. "Mom says Honey's the queen bee there."

Sean could certainly imagine Honey charming every male bee in the yacht club hive. "Flowers couldn't hurt," he said. Though the state Kylie was in, she might be suspicious, rather than flattered, by flowers. "What does your mom need right now? After a long day at the track, what do you think she wants most?"

"Her feet hurt. And she likes to take a bath. Sometimes we eat chocolate bars."

"That's good. We can make that happen." From the schedule Kylie had given him, Sean knew she was attending a sponsor function with Will for another hour. That didn't leave them much time. "Do you still have a key to your mom's room?"

Ryan pulled the keycard from the pocket of his jeans. "Right here."

Sean lurched off the couch, then grabbed his rental car keys. "Let's go."

They found a drugstore a block from Kylie's

hotel. There, they snagged a cart and filled it with creams, bath beads and a foot massager tub. They found a neck pillow filled with lavender-scented beads that could be heated in the microwave. They picked out truffles and a bottle of wine. Being guys, and knowing when to grab opportune moments, they also bought a little junk food for themselves.

Bags in hand, they headed to the hotel and up the elevator to her room. "Should we set everything on the desk?" Sean asked as he surveyed the space.

Ryan, his arms overloaded with the foot tub and neck pillow, struggled to shrug. "I guess."

They arranged their purchases in a sort of pile on the desk, then Ryan decided the bath stuff should be in the bathroom, so he moved those things in there. Stepping back, they eyed their efforts. It wasn't by any means artful or professional, but the thought was clearly evident.

"You've got the note?" Sean asked.

Ryan waved the envelope.

"Set it on top."

They'd signed it, "From the two guys who love you best." Obvious? Definitely. But he and Kylie were past subtlety and taking things slow. He'd figured she'd run in the opposite direction if he told her he was serious, not simply "having fun." Yet he'd lost her anyway.

A new plan was needed. And even if he was taking advice from a ten-year-old and being obvious, he was willing to do that and a great deal more to get her back.

"IT SERIOUSLY says, 'From the two guys who love you best'?"

Tired and completely confused as she sank onto the end of her hotel room bed, Kylie stared at Ryan and Sean's signatures. "I'm reading it word for word off the card," she said to Felicia.

"What does that mean? Well, I mean it's obvious what it means to Ryan, but what about Sean?"

"I have no idea."

"*He* loves you best? The best what? Ex-girlfriend—and I still think you made a mistake there—or best mother of his favorite player? Maybe the best PR rep in racing?"

"I still have no idea."

"Maybe Ryan made up the quote, and Sean signed the card."

"The quote is in Sean's handwriting."

Felicia was silent for a long moment. "What does *that* mean?"

"I have no idea." But the possibilities were darting through her mind. She and Sean had had a fling. He was supposed to move on to his miniskirted hotties after their relationship ended. There were no deep-seated feelings. Love was never a consideration. What was he doing? What was he planning?

Was this some way of getting her to help him find Hilton Branch?

No.

No matter what had gone on between them, she'd calmed down enough in the last few days to realize Sean hadn't used her to solve his case. He *had* gotten access to the track without her help. He hadn't questioned her about Hilton. In fact, he'd helped her and Will when they'd needed him and his expertise. And though she was worried about her job and how the Branch family might perceive her if they found out Sean's role in Hilton's capture, she knew he hadn't seduced her to get information. In a way, it was arrogant of her to think she had any help to give. He was certainly competent enough without her.

He was probably amazing.

But she was holding on to her anger by her fingernails because there were so many other aspects of his job, the man himself and the emotions he stirred up in her that she wasn't ready to face. There were dangers and risks she didn't want to tackle. Not again.

She also wasn't ready to accept the idea that a man like Sean was interested in a real relationship. And, as fun as a fling could be, it simply wasn't enough for her. She was, unfortunately, a forever kind of girl.

"Do *you* have an idea?" she asked Felicia, trying to focus again on the card and its cryptic meaning.

"I think he's been secretly in love with you this entire time."

Her heart jumped, but she forced disbelief into her voice. "Oh, you've *got* to be kidding. Felicia, why—"

"If you dare say anything resembling, 'He's way too young and hot to be seriously interested in me,' I'm going to scream."

"He *is* way too young and hot to be seriously interested in me." When her friend let out only a squeak of aggravation, she considered herself fortunate. "Sean and I are history. It's better for me this way."

Though, at some point, she should probably apologize for her unfounded accusations. She'd planned to earlier. Then she'd seen him, so gorgeous and rebellious, his eyes fiery and seductive, and her well-planned words had fled. He was angry, too. And maybe that was for the best.

"Better for you, how?" Felicia asked, clearly aggravated. "Better for you to be lonely? Or better for you to refuse to take any risks? Or better for you to not get your heart broken again?"

"All three," Kylie said, undaunted by her friend's sarcastic tone.

"You're crazy. He's perfect for you."

"How would you know? You've never even met him."

"I've seen your face when you talk about him."

"The baffled-he's-interested-in-me face, the suspicious face, the intimidated face or the angry face?"

"Kylie" was all Felicia said.

The quiet censure brought Kylie's back up for a second, then she all but collapsed into herself. Her feelings for and about Sean were intense, and she was frankly exhausted. She'd let his smile and easygoing manner seduce her, only to learn he was a bounty hunter whose current case could threaten her job. She'd had one date, started a fling, then crashed back to reality with dizzying speed.

Underneath the anger and worry, though, was

pain. Pain over a man. Hadn't she promised herself she'd never be that vulnerable again? Hadn't she been determined to raise her son, do her job and live quietly alone?

Hadn't she decided *never* to fall in love again?

And yet she found herself teetering dangerously on the edge of that unstable emotion. If Sean wasn't after Hilton Branch, if he hadn't lied, would she have gone over in a matter of weeks? Maybe days?

Probably.

Was Sean on that same cliff? Was that what was at the bottom of his cryptic note?

"Say something," Felicia ordered.

"So it's possible the fling became something more."

"Go on."

Kylie laid back on the bed, staring at the ceiling, searching, not with her eyes but with her heart. "He's really terrific. Smart, fun, considerate. He focuses on me, you know? When he looks at me, I feel like I'm all he's thinking about. Unless Ryan's around, then he manages to focus on both of us."

"And Ryan's crazy about him."

"He tucked him in one night," Kylie said quietly, remembering the night Sean had put Ryan to bed, realizing that was the moment she'd begun to fall for him.

When a man fell for your kid, wasn't it just a matter of time before you fell for him?

"I trusted him with Ryan even when I was furious with him. I never considered canceling the camping trip for them. Shouldn't I have? Shouldn't I be worried that a man I've only known a few weeks is totally responsible for my son?"

"He makes you feel safe," Felicia said. "And since safety is one of your big hang-ups…"

"I don't have—"

"With all the big, bad stuff out there, wouldn't you be glad to have a man who can protect you in the house?"

Kylie's hand tightened around the phone. "I can protect myself just fine, thank you."

"Oh, good grief. That pride of yours is getting on my nerves."

"You don't have a man in the house. Do *you* feel safe?"

"Do you know how fortunate you are to have found somebody like Sean? Do you know how many people are looking for a connection like that?"

You, for one. Kylie was sorry she'd touched that particular nerve with Felicia. Worry and stress was turning her into an insensitive and lousy friend.

"I can't believe you're going to get all weirded out and—"

"I'm not weirded out."

"You so are. Tell you what. When you and your pride screw up this relationship, send Sean my way. I'd sleep even better with him in my apartment."

The jealousy over the image of Sean and Felicia together made her big, bad pride shrink quickly. "We were talking about my feelings for a guy, and now you've got him moving in."

"He's a *keeper,* Kylie. What else are you going to do with him?"

The hot sex in the hotel room was pretty great. But she could see what her friend was trying to do—get her to picture herself with Sean weeks, months and years from now.

And she did see him.

Sitting at her mother's kitchen table, while Honey tried not to be charmed by him, even though she clearly was. Picking her up from work at lunchtime for a romantic hour at his apartment or to actually have lunch. Camping and playing soccer with Ryan.

Then further ahead, to the lake house they both wanted. Would they agree on marble countertops and hardwood floors? A gas fireplace or wood-burning? What trees would they plant in the yard? Would they get a dog or a cat?

Everyday decisions, but for her they were beyond scary.

They were part of the future, after all. A vague place of shadows and light, with no pain or soul-crippling grief. But she also knew there always was and always would be good and bad in the world. Love was all the more precious when surrounded by despair.

At the very least she and Sean needed to talk. She needed to tell him she didn't think he'd used her, and she need to let him apologize.

And, while he was at it, maybe he could explain the dang "love" note.

"So I'll think about calling him," she said to Felicia.

"I get to plan the wedding!" Felicia said, then hung up.

Kylie dropped the phone on the bed and closed her eyes. She wondered if she'd soon be thanking her friend for at least *considering* a peek over that emotional ledge where she was perched, hanging on for dear life to the past and pretending she was secure.

Or would she step over and fall long and hard, landing with a shuddering crash?

CHAPTER THIRTEEN

SEAN STARED at the e-mail on his PDA and reread it for the third time.

Confirmation of Branch boarding outbound Miami flight, destination Nassau, Bahamas. Flight number 2341 due to arrive at 9:42 a.m. eastern today. See attached photo. Make sure I get my reward, buddy.
Lupe

Sean briefly studied the attached picture of a man, who was clearly Hilton Branch—this time wearing a strawberry blond hairpiece—then downloaded the photo to his laptop and printed several copies to the attached printer on his desk.

Bless Lupe, his job at the Miami airport and his somewhat unfair, but convenient, prejudice against the U.S. government. The deportation of Lupe's illegal alien cousin might actually solve his case. And with the bounty money in the bank, Sean could not only pay his observant friend's reward, but maybe hire his cousin and get him a green card.

He packed his laptop quickly and dashed from his office, pausing only long enough to tell Jeremy to book him an immediate flight to Nassau and assure him he'd give him an update later. Since he kept a bag perpetually packed in the back of his jeep, his only remaining obligation was to call Kylie and cancel the camping trip for him and Ryan.

Wincing, he headed toward her house. This was best done in person.

On Sunday after the race, before she'd left for the airport with Will to attend a sponsor event that had come up at the last minute, she'd pulled Sean aside and thanked him for the gift basket. There wasn't time to say much, but she'd smiled at him and squeezed his hand, promising they'd talk soon about all that had happened in the past few days.

Buoyed by her smile, Sean had flown home with Ryan. They'd decided their campaign to soften up Kylie was coming along so well that they made other plans, and one of them was to repeat the camping weekend at Dover. But then Sean had left town to retrieve a witness on another case and hadn't returned home until late last night.

And now, on Thursday afternoon, when he and Ryan were due to leave in mere hours for their trip, he had to cancel.

That couldn't be good.

But he also knew he couldn't let the best lead he'd had to date on Branch slip by. The sooner that guy was behind bars, the sooner he and Kylie could repair what he'd damaged and move on. Hopefully.

If she didn't throw him out after he disappointed her son.

When he reached her house, he swallowed his nerves and approached the front door. Kylie herself answered and gave him a confused half smile. "Are you really early, or did I get the time wrong?"

Her hair was in a ponytail, and she wore white shorts and a navy tank top. He tried not to think about the softness of those long, lean legs but failed in a big way. He was giving up more than his time with Ryan; he was trading an opportunity to see Kylie all weekend.

He knew he had to think beyond the moment, but it wasn't easy.

"I'm early," he said and made himself smile. "Can I talk to you, alone, for a minute?"

She met his gaze briefly, the wonder obvious, then she stepped aside so he could join her in the foyer. "Ryan's out back, so I guess he didn't hear the doorbell. What's up?"

"I can't go camping this weekend."

"Oh." Her gaze settled on his again, and this time it held. "Why?"

"It's Hilton Branch. I've found him. I'm pretty sure, anyway." He slid his hand from her shoulder to her wrist, then grasped her hand. "I'm sorry. You know I don't want to disappoint Ryan, but if I get Hilton, this could all be over." He squeezed her hand and dared to let himself hope. "We could start over and this time—"

She pulled away. "I'll tell Ryan."

He shook his head. "I should tell him."

"Fine."

She turned her back, presumably to lead him to the backyard, but he laid his hands on her shoulders, stopping her. "I'm sorry. I'm so sorry I didn't tell you about my assignment to retrieve Branch. I was so caught up being with you, I thought I could keep my missions separate—winning you and bringing in a fugitive you knew. I was wrong."

"It's more than that, Sean, and you know it."

He had no idea if that was her way of accepting his apology, but at least she wasn't storming away. "I know you're scared. Would it help you to know I am, too?"

Her head whipped toward him. "What makes you think I'm scared?"

"I know you're scared of taking a chance with me." He stroked her cheek and sensed the nerves vibrating just beneath the surface. "Of falling in love again."

She blinked. Then those big blue eyes narrowed. "Is that what you think we're doing, falling in love?"

"I know I am." He leaned toward her, brushed his lips with hers. "I know I *have*."

The worry went away when he touched her. He didn't doubt for a second that they could make it together, that the two of them and Ryan, plus a little Honey, could be a family together. But he knew Kylie hadn't arrived at that secure place yet. Maybe she never would. But that didn't mean he couldn't try—and damn hard.

She licked her lips as she stared at him. "So that's what the note was all about?"

"Of course. And I was trying to get you to see that it's okay to let somebody take care of you every once in a while, that you can count on somebody besides yourself."

"Like I counted on you for this weekend?"

He straightened and dropped his hand by his side. She knew how to throw some pretty painful darts when she was upset. "Why is my having to leave town unexpectedly today any different from you asking me Sunday morning if I could fly back with Ryan, so you and Will could go to that sponsor event directly from New Hampshire?"

"It's not." She sighed. "That wasn't fair. I'm just—"

"Looking for another excuse to be angry at me?"

She angled her head. "Maybe."

"Scared?"

"Yeah, I guess I am."

The back door opened, then slammed before Sean had a chance to reply. "Hi, Coach! Are we leaving early?"

"No, sport," Sean said, ruffling his hair. "I've got some bad news."

Ryan had certainly had bad news before in his life, and Sean hoped, in comparison, this would be little more than a blip. "Okay."

"I can't go this weekend. Something unexpected came up at work, and I have to leave town. I'm on my way to the airport right now." He laid both his hands on Ryan's shoulders, much as he'd done with Kylie, though the boy faced him. "I'm very sorry, and I wouldn't go if it wasn't really, really important. Can I make it up to you another weekend?"

Sean held his breath, then let it out as Ryan slowly nodded. "Sure. We'll have other weekends."

Sean glanced at Kylie, whose face was blank. "I guess we will."

"It seems everything's settled," she said, her tone forced with politeness. "Excuse me. I need to make sure Honey can watch Ryan this weekend."

As she walked down the hall, Sean moved fast to catch up with her. "My brother and sister-in-law will be here," he said. "Ryan could stay with them and hang out with Patrick."

"He's *my* responsibility. I'll find somebody for him to stay with."

"Let me help."

"Thanks, but no." She turned away, continuing down the hall.

For the first time in his career, Sean was tempted to say the hell with an assignment and go after her. He clenched his fists by his sides and fought the battle between desire and responsibility.

"Is Mom mad?" Ryan asked quietly from behind him.

"I'm not sure," he answered, frustrated and worried.

"She liked the stuff we put in her room."

"So she said." He shook off his troubling thoughts and gave Ryan his full attention. "Don't worry, buddy. It'll be fine." He glanced at his watch and winced. "I need to get going. I'll call you when I get back, and we'll set up another camping weekend. With a no-cancellation guarantee."

"Okay."

"Ryan, go clean your room," Kylie said, appearing at the end of the hall. "Honey's going with us. Camping is back on."

"Cool!" Ryan's face lit up with a wide grin. He took off running toward the stairs. "See ya, Coach!"

Kylie's gaze shifted to Sean. "You are an extremely lucky man."

Sean tried for a small smile. "All I need now is you."

She held his gaze for another minute, but he had no idea what she was thinking. "Go. Go get Hilton, already."

He nodded, then turned and walked out the door, unsure whether the exasperation in her voice was encouraging or not. Either way, he knew one thing for certain—he wasn't coming back without Hilton Branch in custody.

Kylie lounged in the crook of the sofa and sipped iced tea as she watched Honey and Ryan in their latest video game battle.

Since Ryan had Friday off from school they'd driven up Thursday night in the motor home and settled into their camping spot. Then, while Kylie worked this morning and during qualifying, her mother and son had taken Honey's lime green sports car, which they towed behind the motor home, to the store for fresh provisions. After qualifying was over, they'd grilled chicken, baked potatoes and made salads.

Kylie was full and content, along with being relieved she didn't have to drive to a hotel and spend the night by herself, flipping around the TV channels and missing her family. Absently watching Ryan narrowly pass two cars on the video's track, she continued the mental game she'd been playing ever since Felicia had tried to convince her to take her relationship with Sean seriously.

If it wasn't for the Branch case, he would certainly be in the mix of the race. Or bugging them to switch to the soccer game. Earlier, he would have insisted on cooking the chicken, assuring her, with a quick, teasing kiss, that grilling was man's work. Later, they'd cuddle on the sofa, her leaning back against his chest, maybe while they all watched a DVD. A family hanging out together on a Friday night.

A happy family.

She swallowed the lump in her throat that rose over the memory of having that before, only to have it destroyed in the blink of an eye. Was she crazy to chance happiness again? Or was she crazy not to?

"That's the second time you've beaten me," Honey grumbled.

"Everybody's gotta win sometime," Ryan said with a shrug.

"You're getting help." Honey narrowed her eyes. "Will's helping you."

"Good grief, Mom," Kylie said before her son

could do more than flush. "What if Will did give him a few pointers?"

"He's a *professional*," Honey said indignantly.

Kylie rolled her eyes. "You're just a sore loser."

Ryan giggled. "Maybe we could find a boat racing game, Honey. Then you could ask one of the captains for help."

Honey tipped up her chin. "Don't think I won't."

As she walked into the kitchen, muttering under her breath and no doubt planning to approach one of the racing champions for a tutoring lesson of her own, Kylie was grateful that though she was certainly competitive, she hadn't inherited that trait to her mother's extreme. Shifting her attention to her son, she said, "Shower time."

"Aw, Mom…"

"You can play some more afterward," she assured him. "After all that running around you did today, I don't want you conking out on me before you're clean."

"It's not even ten o'clock," he grumbled, though he rose and headed down the hall.

"Haven't you ever heard of the concept of letting a kid win every once in a while?" she asked her mother.

"No," she said, her head ducked into the fridge, "I don't believe I'm familiar with that one."

"There's a shock."

Honey walked back into the living room with a glass of straw-colored wine. She extended it toward Kylie. "Take this. We need to talk."

"About?"

"Sean."

Kylie took it.

Honey went back into the kitchen briefly, returning with her own wineglass. "I've been giving your relationship a lot of thought."

Great. She had Felicia as an encouraging crew chief and Honey as a skeptical NASCAR official, itching to throw a caution. She was wondering whether she should try to escape or pretend to listen intently, then simply tell her mother she'd think about what she'd said. Then she tuned into what Honey was actually saying.

"…should go for it."

"Go for what?" she asked, completely confused and wondering what she'd missed while chasing her rambling thoughts.

"Sean."

"Go for…"

"Well, really, you don't have to go anywhere. He'll come to you. He's completely crazy about you, and while he *is* a bit young, I've realized that's just what you need. You need somebody exciting, full of promise and hope." She sipped her wine, then grinned at her over the rim. "And when you get a bit saggy around the middle or baggy under the eyes, there's always Dr. Paulson."

"Let me get this straight. You *want* me to date Sean?"

"Not for long. You need to marry him pretty quickly. You can't let some twenty-something chick come along and steal your man."

Kylie took a gulp of wine, then set her glass aside. Having a super hip mom had its overwhelming and odd moments, but this one was a real doozy. "Steal my man?"

Honey pursed her lips. "Come to think of it, you might not have to worry about that. He's so in love with you, I can't imagine him looking at another woman, much less letting one cart him off."

Kylie tried to swallow again, but this time a lump clogged her throat. "In love with me?"

"Sure. You love him, too." She patted her hand while Kylie shook her head. "It's really sweet," she continued despite Kylie's silent denial. "You know I loved Matt, and Sean is so different from him, but still, well, perfect for you somehow."

"Mom, a lot has happened in the last few days." She didn't want to worry her about the bounty hunting, but she had to make Honey see that she couldn't be in love with Sean. Or maybe it was herself she had to convince. The silly daydreams she'd been having about them had been fun, but she wasn't ready to see them as reality yet. Maybe she *could*, but right now, the drop off that cliff was too steep and high, and she'd discovered she was scared of heights. "Sean and I have some serious issues to—"

Honey waved her hand vaguely. "Sure you do. All couples do. You'll work them out. He'll make a wonderful father for Ryan."

As if the whole matter was decided.

Her eyes brightened suddenly. "Maybe *he* can give me some tips for the racing game."

Good grief. Kylie tried another approach. "When did you decide all this?"

"It's been coming around for a while. I'd figured out his feelings a couple of weeks ago, of course, but then it really struck me that you felt the same way when I saw how miserable you were after you two fought last Wednesday night."

"How do you know we had a fight?"

"From Ryan, of course."

Oh, joy. Her mother and her son had discussed her love life. Well, hopefully not the sex part. "He stood Ryan up for this weekend," she said, suddenly inspired of a way to get Honey off the Sean-is-perfect bandwagon. How was she supposed to resist the advice of her mother, her son *and* her best friend?

"For something obviously important," Honey said confidently. "Just what does he do for this security company, anyway? He's been a little vague about that." Considering, she angled her head, then grabbed Kylie's hand. "You don't think he's really a secret government spy or something, do you? Maybe he's been called to Prague by the president and, right this very minute, he's wearing a tux and saving the world from a nefarious terrorist plot."

Leave it to Honey to see the adventure, not the danger.

Forget not worrying her. The woman *needed* to be worried. She needed to realize this relationship between her and Sean was impossible. Called to Prague by the president. *Really.*

"He's a bounty hunter," she said shortly and waited for the explosion of outrage.

"Oh." Honey's face flushed pink with pleasure. "Oh, my." She waved her hand, fanning herself. "How…exciting. I knew there was something just a little bit bad about him. Though bad in a good way, if you know what I mean. I don't suppose he has a much older brother, uncle or cousin?"

Kylie rubbed her temples. "Mom!"

"Oh, stop your worrying." Honey hugged her to her side. "Love isn't always painful, you know," she said, turning serious.

"I know." Or at least she remembered vaguely.

"And grief eases with time. You don't have to feel guilty for finding love and happiness again."

"I'm scared," she admitted, tears gathering her eyes. It felt so nice to lean against somebody she loved and trusted implicitly for just a few minutes.

"We all are."

"Not you."

"Sure I am." Honey rocked her, much as she'd done when Kylie was a child and life's disappointments had knocked her for a loop. "When I lost your father, I lost my life partner." She sighed, but the sound wasn't sad. It was more of an acceptance. "I'll never replace him, so I don't even begin to try. That doesn't mean I can't have fun trying."

"And if one day you meet a captain who makes your world stop and your heart swell?"

"I'll grab him with both hands and refuse to let

go." Honey kissed the top of her head. "Grab hold of Sean, sweetie. It's no fun to fall in love alone."

PUMPED BY A HOT TIP from a skycap at the Nassau airport, Sean leaped into a cab. "Surf and Sand Hotel," he said to the driver. "If we get there fast, I've got fifty American dollars for you."

They got there fast.

Though the ride had been a bit like a harrowing trip through Manhattan with a bold and experienced NYC cabbie, Sean was grinning as he got out, slipped the driver his fare and the fifty, then slung his duffel bag over his shoulder.

He nodded at the valet who pulled back the brass-handled door and felt a moment's bitterness toward Branch as he walked into the posh lobby. The hotel was off-the-scale upscale. Luxury spilled out of colorful hothouse flowers, potted palms, towering ceilings, tastefully elegant furnishings, plush carpeting and the professionally dressed and polished staff.

While his sons had scrambled for racing sponsorships and his wife desperately tried to gather her dignity and restore the family reputation, Hilton the Patriarch had been living the high life. *Creep*.

Sean approached the reservations desk and gave the dusky skinned female clerk a flirtatious smile. "Recognize this guy?" he asked, discretely extending the Miami airport photo of Branch.

Never looking at the picture, she met his gaze with dark eyes full of polite refusal. "It's the hotel's firm policy not to comment on the comings and goings of our guests. Do you have a reservation?"

"I need to find this man. Could you look again, please? You don't have to say anything," he said, his voice low. "Just nod if you've seen him."

She sighed, but glanced at the picture. Her eyes lit briefly with recognition, then she looked at Sean and shook her head. "It's our firm policy—"

"Yeah, sure. Sorry I bothered you about it." The flicker of recognition was enough. "Do you have any available rooms?"

"We do." Her fingers clicked across her keyboard. "How many nights?"

"One." *For now, anyway.* The hotel was big, but Branch had been bold enough so far that Sean didn't think he'd be hiding in his room for long.

He was so close, and there was too much at stake. He'd find his target. Soon.

He simply wouldn't accept anything less.

After storing his bag in his room, he headed to the elaborate pool he'd seen from the fifteenth-floor view out his window. He sat at the bar and ordered a beer, more to be inconspicuous and sociable than to drink. He glanced around at the happy faces and bodies glistening under the Caribbean sun and fought back both grief and hope.

If he and Kylie were here together, he could imagine talking her into one of those fruity, brightly colored drinks, decorated with an umbrella and a pineapple wedge. They'd play in the water and lay on the beach. They'd stroll and have a quiet dinner.

Later, he'd tumble her onto the bed in their room.

"Beer's cold, yeah?" the bartender asked, breaking into his fantasy.

"Yeah." Sean took another sip. "Thanks."

Despite his ridiculously bright and flowered shirt, Marc—so said his orange plastic nametag—had sharp, nearly black eyes and musical accent. "You need anything, Cali-man. I'm here for you." He flashed a bright smile against his dark skin.

"Cali-man?"

"You a surfer, right? Or maybe one of those triathletes?"

Based on that sharp gaze and the memory of Kylie making the same observation, Sean made a calculated decision. "I'm a P.I.," he said, showing him his license. "I need to find a guy. You help, I'll tip generously."

"How generous?"

"A hundred now. A hundred if you call me when you see him."

Marc studied him for a long moment, then nodded. "Works for me." He laid his hand, palm down on the bar, and Sean slipped him the hundred, which he pocketed. "Who's the guy?"

Explaining Branch was wanted by the American government was an extremely bad idea. One, because many islanders tended to have a live-and-let-live attitude, and two, because sharp islanders might see the profits in being an informant—and the monetary reward that might follow. Still, Sean didn't consider their transaction a con. He figured he was saving the guy a lot of aggravation and time. The money they exchanged would be quick and much easier obtained than waiting for the government red tape to unwind on any federal reward years down the road.

"Him," Sean said, laying the photo of Branch faceup on the bar.

"Haven't seen 'im," Marc said after a moment. "But I be lookin' out for you, Cali-man."

"I'm in room 1523. If you see him, call me."

Marc promised he would call, Sean finished his beer, then wandered around the pool and down the beach. He looked for Branch and thought about Kylie. He questioned several more employees and a couple of guests, but had no luck with an actual sighting of the man in question.

Trolling the shops in the hotel, he paused outside the entrance to an elegant jewelry store. Diamonds, sapphires and rubies glimmered invitingly from the glass cases, encouraging the idle rich and/or bored to scoop up their contents.

The salesperson on duty, an elegantly dressed Asian man named Ki, hadn't seen Branch, but he invited Sean to peruse his high-quality merchandise.

Frustrated, yet knowing he simply needed to wait for his web of informants to contact him about a Branch sighting, Sean skeptically studied the sparkling contents of the shop. He used the loupe Ki gave him, and with his training in recognizing fenced and fake gems, he realized the jewelry wasn't overpriced, or of the questionable quality that normally dominated a resort hotel boutique.

Before he knew it, he was examining loose stones. Loose stones that Ki could put into the setting of his choice for the lady in his life.

As he studied a particularly stunning emerald-cut diamond, his earlier fantasies returned. He imagined standing on the sugary beach and slipping the ring on Kylie's finger as the brilliant sun disappeared beyond the sea.

"I want it," he said to Ki.

They engaged in a quick and civilized negotiation over the price, ending with Ki promising to have the diamond set by the following morning. Sean's heart raced as he passed over his credit card. He might be crazy for pushing his and Kylie's relationship forward with this kind of suddenness, but he couldn't find any regret. She'd probably turn him down, but at least she'd finally realize he wasn't playing games and having a fling.

He was *serious*. Completely and utterly serious about spending the rest of his life with her and Ryan.

He wound up ordering dinner from room service, staring down at the pool and beach from his window and watching the sun set, longing for Kylie. He alternately wished for Branch to put up a good, physical fight so he could release his aggression, and for Branch to come along quietly, so they could get this whole damn thing over with.

After making one last loop around the property, he went back to his room, laid on the bed and stared at the ceiling.

He must have fallen asleep at some point, since

he woke with a sudden start at the ringing of the phone beside the bed.

"Hey, Cali-man. This is Marc at the pool bar."

Sean scrubbed his hand down his face, sat up and struggled to wake up. "Yeah?"

"I spotted your guy. He ordered a rum and Coke."

Wide awake, Sean jumped out of bed. "Where is he now?"

"Sitting at a table in my bar, flirting with Roseen."

"Roseen?"

"She's my waitress." He paused. "And my woman. Can you come get him now?"

Sean smiled wide and hard. "On my way."

He raced out of his room and downstairs. Before he walked through the lobby, he forced his excitement to calm and rolled his shoulders. Striding with a casualness that belied his anticipation, he walked toward the poolside bar. He saw his target and, apparently, Roseen, a curvy, Latina woman with bold red lips.

At least Branch had good taste in ladies.

He approached Marc, pealed off another hundred and slipped it to the bartender. He hoped the guy and Roseen had a serious reunion party with it. "Nice doin' business with ya, Cali-man," Marc said quietly with a nod of thanks.

Sean moved on toward Branch's table. "Roseen, Marc needs to see you."

As the waitress slipped away, Sean faced his quarry. The man who'd eluded local police, the federal government, bank officials, friends, family, associates and, most impressively, the media, for months sat before him, a sweating plastic cup in his hand, a bad, reddish blond wig on his head, a diamond pinky ring on his left hand, a challenging light in his eyes.

"If you're here to offer me free Jet Ski lessons, don't bother." He sipped his drink. "And send Roseen back over, would ya?"

Smiling, Sean leaned against the table. "Good morning, Mr. Branch," he said, and had the pleasure of watching every ounce of color drain out of the other man's face. "My name is Arthur Treadway, and the only free thing I'm offering is a complimentary ride to jail."

CHAPTER FOURTEEN

HE SHOULD HAVE taken him back to Texas.

Watching Branch suck down two rum and Cokes in the last hour, Sean was already questioning his moment of compassion. But then his sympathy wasn't for Branch, who was mostly a selfish jerk, but for Will, who deserved to face the father who'd betrayed him.

Plus, his weak moment had included a bit of self-indulgence. He needed to get to Dover and explain everything in person to Will. He needed to see Kylie and claim the love of his life. In the meantime, Branch could cool his heels in jail in Charlotte until the feds, his family and whoever else came to call.

As his jumper raised his hand to, yet again, punch the flight attendant call button for another drink, Sean grabbed his wrist. "No more drinks."

"If you think I'm going to jail sober, you're crazy."

Compassion was a dangerous emotion.

Sighing, knowing it might be the last decent buzz Branch had for a long, long time, Sean unbuckled his seat belt and rose. He walked down the aisle toward the single flight attendant of the small commercial jet, handed her a twenty and asked for two sampler-size bottles of rum and a can of Coke.

"What'd he do?" she whispered as he took the provisions.

The onboard personnel were apprised of his mission simply because he had to have a top-level clearance to bring a firearm and a handcuffed man on board the plane. As long as he had that security pass, and the felon wasn't considered dangerous, the airline people were usually glad to have him along for the ride. It had to shake up the monotony of flying around with vacationers and people in suits every day.

"Stole money from a bank," Sean said.

Eyes wide, she cast a glance down the aisle. "Like in a ski mask?"

"Like with an illegally shielded foreign account." He laid his hand briefly on her shoulder. "Don't worry. He's not dangerous."

She handed him a couple of packages of crackers, then Sean went back to his seat. After handing the snack and drinks to Branch, he settled back with his *Guns & Ammo* magazine. It was a prop, since Sean's interest in guns was minimal. He trained with them and knew how to use them, as was necessary for his job, but he didn't give them any importance beyond that.

But the magazine screamed *bad ass* to a guy like Branch, and Sean had learned over the years intimidation was a good tool in keeping the peace.

"You just *had* to be a big man and use the handcuffs, didn't you?" Branch said a few minutes later.

The rum had obviously made him bold, even if his speech was a bit slurred.

"Get used to them," Sean advised, not looking up from his magazine.

"I should be treated with dignity. I'm an important man."

"Yeah. I bet your name will be all over CNN by tonight."

"After the glory, aren't you?" Branch blustered with a smug smile. "Gonna get your name on the news, thanks to me."

"Nope. Nobody will ever know who brought you in except the people who paid me to. I get my bounty, the feds get you, and I disappear into the wind."

Branch sipped his drink silently. "Who was that?" he asked finally. "Who hired you?"

"Bank investors. Don't mess with people's money, Branch. They tend to get annoyed."

Branch licked his lips, cast a glance at his drink, then back at Sean. "I've got lots of money."

Sean flipped a page in his magazine. "So I hear."

"If you let me go, I could, you know, make it worth your while."

Sean looked over at him. "A bribe?"

Obviously sensing when a deal went south quick, Branch backpedaled. "You're not a cop. That isn't a crime. You can't—"

Sean held up his hand to stop the excuse parade. "I don't want your money."

"Why not?"

Sean leaned toward him, his gaze hard as it drilled into Branch's. "I realize this is a novel concept for a man like you, but I didn't *earn* that money. Neither did you. I don't want it."

"What do you want?" Branch asked desperately.

Sean had no intention of taking his money, but there was something he wanted to know. "What was in the lockbox?"

"What lockbox?"

"The one you stole from Will's motor home."

Branch took another drink and set his plastic cup on his tray table. "How the devil could you possibly know about that?"

Sean shrugged. "I know. What was in it?"

"Why should I tell you?" Branch asked defensively.

"Because I didn't slug you before I cuffed you."

"Gee, thanks."

"Because I'm your link to your sons."

Branch's head whipped toward him. "My boys?"

"I can get word to them about where you'll be held. I can bring them to see you. If they want to," he added when Branch perked up.

"Identification," Branch said finally. "ID and fake credit cards. I have several sets to get me in and out of the country."

So Will's discretion had helped his father, after all. "You took a big chance. He could have given the box to the cops."

"I raised my boys right," Branch said indignantly.

Sean studied him and was even more disappointed in the man. "To defend their lying, cheating father even when he doesn't deserve it?"

Branch scowled. "I don't like you."

"Then we're even. I don't like you, either."

The remainder of the flight was silent. When they arrived at the terminal, two local police detectives in plain clothes Sean had called were there to greet them at the gate. He wondered if Branch would appreciate the dignity the *important man* had been afforded.

While the rest of the passengers filed off the plane, they waited in their seats. Rising after the last passenger had departed, Sean pulled his cell phone from his coat pocket, and the jewelry case also resting there tumbled onto the floor.

He scooped it up as Branch awkwardly scooted out of his seat, his cuffed hands in front of him. "What's that?" he asked, his eyes wide. "Some kind of bug? You can't record anything I say without my lawyer present."

Actually, since he wasn't a cop, he could. But he didn't have the patience to argue with Branch about legalities at the moment.

He flipped open the lid of the case, revealing the two-carat, emerald-cut diamond that Ki had set. "It's not a bug. I'm going to ask my girlfriend to marry me." He paused, gazing down at the sparkling stone. "Actually, she's my ex-girlfriend."

"You're proposing to your *ex*-girlfriend?" Branch shook his head. "And you think *I* got problems."

SATURDAY NIGHT in Dover, Kylie sat on the sofa in the motor home as she had the previous night. After a glass of wine, she was sleepy and comfortable, reading a book while Ryan watched a favorite movie on TV. Honey had disappeared into her bedroom a while back to talk on the phone to her latest flame.

Her cell phone rang, startling her. Noting Will's number on the screen, she answered it with a sigh. Emergencies, which were the only reason to call her after ten o'clock, did not include requests for a run to the local fast food drive-thru. She prepared herself to turn down those pleas as she answered.

"My dad's in custody," he said in a rush instead.

"I—*Oh*." Her mind jumped to Sean and prayed he'd been the one to bring him in and that he wasn't hurt in the process. "When? How? Is he okay?"

"He's fine. Could you come over? I'll tell you all about it."

"Yeah. Sure. Be right there." She yanked the band from her ponytail, releasing her hair. Rolling off the sofa, she walked to the back of the motor home and knocked on Honey's door. When her mother answered, Kylie said simply, "Hilton Branch has been found."

"Alive?"

"Apparently. I need to go over to Will's. Can you watch Ryan?"

"Sure. Go. And bring back all the details."

The press release she'd prepared already running through her head, Kylie took two minutes to apply lip gloss and change into jeans, though she left on her comfy T-shirt. She had no idea who else Will had called, but figured if anybody expected polish from her past 10:00 p.m., they were doomed to disappointment.

After kissing Ryan good-night, she strode quickly through the fan-filled motor home parking area and headed toward the drivers' and owners' lot. It was close to the garage area, surrounded by a secure fence and a savvy guard, who'd apparently been alerted to her arrival, as he passed her straight through.

Had Sean found him? she wondered as she rushed toward Will's motor home. *Had the cops?*

If Sean had found him and their relationship was brought to light, she was going to have some major explaining to do. After her boss had struggled to gain control of her PR company and get sponsorships for Will and his brother, Kylie knew she'd be out on her butt if she'd ticked off their clients or had done anything to jeopardize her company's reputation.

But Kylie still hoped Sean had. The bounty was important to his business, and, more than that, to his pride.

And you claim you aren't in love with him?

She wanted him to succeed, even if it jeopardized her job. If that wasn't love, she didn't know what was.

Sighing and shoving her personal issues aside as she reached Will's motor home, she wiped her damp hands on her jeans, then knocked. He called for her to come in, so she opened the door and strode inside.

And found Sean sitting on the couch.

"Hi," he said.

Heart pounding at the sight of him, as well as its

meaning, Kylie cast a nervous glance toward Will, who was standing in the kitchen, smiling at her. "Um, hi."

"He knows," Sean said, bringing her attention back to him.

"And you thought I'd be mad Arthur was the one trying to bring Dad in?" Will asked her. "Come on, Kylie. Give me a little more credit for sense than that."

"I— You brought him in?" she asked Sean.

"I did."

Twin spurts of pride and relief shot through her. She smiled widely. As she met Sean's gaze, her heart leaped at the center-of-his-world focus, the concern and the emotions she saw there. All for her. "Congratulations."

"He's in Charlotte," Will said. "He brought him to Charlotte, so all of us—Bart, my brother Sawyer, my sister Penny and me can see him before…" he trailed off.

Before the FBI got its hooks into him and sent him to prison for twenty years. She crossed to Will and gave him a hug. "Are you relieved?"

"Yeah, but it's Arthur you should be hugging," Will said.

"I'll get to him. Are you sure you're okay?" She searched his face. "About your dad's capture? About me introducing you to Bounty Hunter Guy over there?"

"I'm fine." He kissed her cheek. "Don't be such a worrier."

"I'm trying."

"Keep at it. So, you guys have a lot to discuss," Will said, winking at Sean as he headed toward the door. "I'm going over to Bart's. We've got to figure out when we can all go see Dad together. Then we have to tell my mom. Not looking forward to that part." He turned back just before he walked down the steps. "Thanks, man."

Nodding, Sean rose to his feet. "Sure."

When the door closed behind Will, the silence was deafening. But as Kylie looked at Sean, strong, confident and gorgeous, the nerves and worries she'd held on to for so many days and weeks faded away. He was back, unhurt, and had done right by Will and his family.

The love she'd been fighting since the moment they'd met rolled over her like a tidal wave. And she didn't feel as if she'd jumped off a cliff at all. Instead, she felt exhilarated by the possibilities of more waves in the future and calm about her decision.

Her mom was right. Sean was perfect.

Felicia was right. He was a keeper.

Her son was right. He was the coolest guy around.

She moved toward him, throwing her arms around his neck and holding him tight. "I'm so proud of you."

"I love you," Sean said.

She leaned back, staring at him.

He kissed her briefly. "Sorry. I had a much more romantic speech planned." He cupped her cheek. "But I've been holding it in so long, it kind of burst out."

"I know the feeling. I love you, too."

Beneath her fingertips, his heart raced. "You do?"

She angled her head. "Being the clever detective you are, I figured you already knew."

"Of course I knew. I just thought I'd have to drag it out of you."

"Because I'm stubborn and difficult."

"Naturally." He kissed her. "And smart and beautiful." He kissed her again. "Generous and compassionate." Another kiss, longer and thorough enough to have Kylie's head spinning. "And mine."

She trailed her fingers through his hair. "I guess I have a boyfriend again."

He grinned. "You could have a lot more than that."

Then, to her utter shock, he dropped to one knee in front of her, pulled a blue velvet box from his pocket and opened it, revealing a huge diamond ring. "Kylie Palmer, will you marry me?"

"I—" Mouth dry and at a complete loss for words, she searched his gaze, finding all the love and devotion any couple needed to make a life together. "Are you sure we're ready for marriage?"

"Yes. I'm asking for a lifelong commitment *and* undying love."

She smiled with remembrance. "To get me to go out with you the first time, you said you weren't."

"I know, but I had to take what you'd give me at the time. Though I knew even then you weren't the fling type. You're a forever kind of woman."

He never thought of her as temporary or a flingee. The thought made her warm and secure in the knowledge that she was his one and only. And always had been.

The future shimmered before her. Sean would always do crazy, impulsive things, and she'd always try to be the voice of reason. Then she'd look into his eyes and see his determination. He'd smile, and she'd cave.

Just like now.

"Okay, but no chasing criminals on our honeymoon."

"Deal." His grin burst wide, he slid the ring on her finger, then jumped to his feet. He picked her up and spun her around. "How's Thanksgiving at the beach sound?"

She gasped for air. "Soon. It sounds really soon."

He set her down and cupped her face in his hands. "I guess I'll have to ask your friend Felicia's permission for wedding dates and details."

"First, we have to clear everything through Honey and Ryan."

"Ryan already knows," he said casually, taking her hand and leading her outside.

"How's that?"

"Well, he knows I love you and that I wanted us to all be a family. He said as long as he didn't have to wear a tie to the ceremony, I had his permission to marry you."

The boy was a born negotiator. "When did you guys make that deal?"

"Last weekend."

"We were broken up last weekend."

"Yeah, well, Ryan and I were riding high on hope and overcooked hot dogs."

Holding hands, they walked through the camping areas toward Honey's motor home.

"You never did say. Where did you find Hilton?" Kylie asked.

"Nassau."

"So he was on an island after all." She bumped his shoulder with hers. "How much is the bounty for somebody like that?"

"Two million dollars."

"Good freakin'—" She ground to a halt and goggled at him. "Seriously?"

He grinned. "Seriously."

"How much of that do you get personally?"

"Greedy now, are you?"

"Sorry. Lake house fantasies. It doesn't matter. I'm sure you had a lot of expenses and stuff."

He led her to Honey's door. "Three quarters of it goes to the balloon payment due on the loan where my family business is located. The rest is mine. Minus the ten-thousand-dollar reward for Lupe, the observant Miami airport employee."

She did the quick math. "That's almost five hundred thousand dollars left."

"It certainly is." He stroked her cheek. "When do you want to start building?"

* * * * *

*For more thrill-a-minute romances set
against the exciting backdrop of the
NASCAR world, don't miss*

*RISKY MOVES by Gina Wilkins
Available in November*

For a sneak peek, just turn the page!

"So, Tobey, how do you feel about replacing the man you claim taught you everything you know about being a crew chief?"

Tobey Harris squirmed a little in his chair, uncomfortable with the line of questioning introduced by the very attractive woman facing him from a matching chair. "I have nothing but the greatest respect for Neil Sanchez. He's a great guy and I wish him success in whatever he chooses to pursue next."

"Can you tell our listeners more about why he was fired? It had to have been serious for team owner Dawson Ritter to dump the established crew chief this late in the season."

Tobey felt his eyes narrow in irritation. Remembering his onlookers, he tried to keep his emotions out of his voice and expression when he replied, "Neil left the team through mutual agreement, for reasons of his own. As I said, I think he's a great guy. Perhaps you'd like to talk about the upcoming race now?"

His interviewer nodded. Her amber-brown eyes

were focused intently on his face when she asked the next question. "All right, about the race. It will be the first you've called as a crew chief. How does the rest of the team feel about answering to a young man who was the crew chief's assistant less than a week ago? Especially a baby-faced guy who looks barely older than a teenager, himself?"

A few onlookers snickered. Feeling his cheeks warm, Tobey scowled. "Oh, come on—"

"Answer the question, Tobey," a man's voice ordered from the shadows behind the bright lights focused on Tobey's face. "You're going to hear worse."

Sighing loudly, Tobey struggled for patience. This was just a practice interview, he reminded himself. His owner and driver wanted to see how he would conduct himself when hit with the really tough questions. He would prove to them that he could handle whatever was thrown at him—not that he had expected anything quite like this.

"I've served as Neil's assistant for two years, including last year, when our team won the NASCAR Sprint Cup Series Championship. I've been active in stock car racing for most of my life, and I've trained for this position for ten years. I have received the team's full support during this past week, and I have no doubt that we can take the No. 427 car to Victory Lane next weekend."

"Gonna have to take that chip off your shoulder, son," Dawson Ritter advised, stepping out of the shadows with driver Kent Grosso at his side. "You knew when you took this job that there was going to be talk about you replacing Neil. About your lack of experience as a crew chief. And about that baby face of yours, for that matter. You have to let it slide off your back and not get you riled up."

"I can handle it, sir," Tobey assured his employer. "Doesn't mean I have to like it, though."

With a snort of sympathy, Dawson clapped Tobey's shoulder. "Can't blame you for that. I haven't enjoyed this past week much, myself. But we'll all stick together and we'll get through this."

"Yes, sir."

There was nothing he wanted more than to justify the older man's faith in him. Dawson had taken a risk in promoting an untried crew chief. Tobey was all too well aware that Kent was worried about the next race. It wasn't going to be easy for the driver to put his full faith in a new crew chief this late in the season.

That so-called practice interview hadn't helped, Tobey thought resentfully as Kent and Dawson moved away, talking in low voices.

He whirled toward the woman who hovered behind him. "Thanks a lot, Amy. You made me look like an idiot in front of Kent and Mr. Ritter. Not to mention the other guys standing around watching."

Amy Barber, Kent's PR representative, had the grace to look just a little rueful, even as she defended her actions. "Dawson told me to be tough with you. You need to be prepared for anything the media asks you—and trust me, I could have been harsher."

It wasn't easy to be angry with Amy. Her wide-set, golden-brown eyes met his gaze evenly, and the expression on her pretty oval face was conciliatory. Not apologetic exactly, since she believed she had been doing exactly what she was supposed to do—but not confrontational, either. She apparently understood why he was annoyed by the questions she had asked. After all, that had been the purpose of her asking them.

Still…

"That 'baby face' remark was below the belt," he growled, shoving his hands into his pockets. "I'm doing my best to convince Kent that I'm ready to take charge of the team, and you probably undermined any progress I might have made this week."

"I was doing my job," she replied quietly. "And you should get used to it, because you're going to be seeing a great deal of me for the rest of this season."

He felt something tighten in his stomach in response to that…promise? Warning?

Funny to think that he'd spent the past few months occasionally fantasizing about seeing more of Amy Barber.

He supposed this situation proved the old adage. *Be careful what you wish for.*

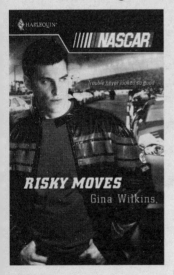

Love Inspired.
HISTORICAL

INSPIRATIONAL HISTORICAL ROMANCE

Years after being wrenched from Alice Shepard's life due to his lowborn status, Nicholas Tennant returns to London. Now wealthy and influential, he seeks revenge on Alice and her family. Alice is now a beautiful, grown woman and a loving single mother, and Nicholas cannot deny his feelings for her. Can he abandon his thirst for revenge and become the man most worthy of her love?

Look for

A Man Most Worthy

by

RUTH AXTELL MORREN

Available October
wherever books are sold.

www.SteepleHill.com

Steeple
Hill®

LIH82797

REQUEST YOUR FREE BOOKS!

2 FREE NOVELS PLUS 2 FREE GIFTS!

SPECIAL EDITION®

Life, Love and Family!

YES! Please send me 2 FREE Silhouette Special Edition® novels and my 2 FREE gifts (gifts are worth about $10). After receiving them, if I don't wish to receive any more books, I can return the shipping statement marked "cancel." If I don't cancel, I will receive 6 brand-new novels every month and be billed just $4.24 per book in the U.S. or $4.99 per book in Canada, plus 25¢ shipping and handling per book and applicable taxes, if any*. That's a savings of at least 15% off the cover price! I understand that accepting the 2 free books and gifts places me under no obligation to buy anything. I can always return a shipment and cancel at any time. Even if I never buy another book from Silhouette, the two free books and gifts are mine to keep forever.

235 SDN EEYU   335 SDN EEY6

Name	(PLEASE PRINT)	
Address		Apt. #
City	State/Prov.	Zip/Postal Code

Signature (if under 18, a parent or guardian must sign)

Mail to the **Silhouette Reader Service:**
IN U.S.A.: P.O. Box 1867, Buffalo, NY 14240-1867
IN CANADA: P.O. Box 609, Fort Erie, Ontario L2A 5X3

Not valid to current subscribers of Silhouette Special Edition books.

Want to try two free books from another line?
Call 1-800-873-8635 or visit www.morefreebooks.com.

* Terms and prices subject to change without notice. N.Y. residents add applicable sales tax. Canadian residents will be charged applicable provincial taxes and GST. Offer not valid in Quebec. This offer is limited to one order per household. All orders subject to approval. Credit or debit balances in a customer's account(s) may be offset by any other outstanding balance owed by or to the customer. Please allow 4 to 6 weeks for delivery. Offer available while quantities last.

Your Privacy: Silhouette is committed to protecting your privacy. Our Privacy Policy is available online at www.eHarlequin.com or upon request from the Reader Service. From time to time we make our lists of customers available to reputable third parties who may have a product or service of interest to you. If you would prefer we not share your name and address, please check here. ☐

SSE08

Love Inspired
SUSPENSE
RIVETING INSPIRATIONAL ROMANCE

REUNION REVELATIONS

Secrets surface when old friends—
and foes—get together.

Look for these six riveting Reunion Revelations stories!

Hidden in the Wall
by VALERIE HANSEN
January 2008

Missing Persons
by SHIRLEE McCOY
February 2008

Don't Look Back
by MARGARET DALEY
March 2008

In His Sights
by CAROL STEWARD
April 2008

A Face in the Shadows
by LENORA WORTH
May 2008

Final Justice
by MARTA PERRY
June 2008

Available wherever books are sold.

Steeple
Hill®

LISRRLIST